The Day I'll Never Forget

By Peter May

Dedicated to Marian.
A wife and a mother who dedicated her
lifetime selflessly to her family.

THE DAY I'LL NEVER FORGET

It was a lovely day in the middle of September 1978; George Stevenson is taking a Sunday afternoon walk along a country lane with his grandson, Simon. It was his 16th birthday.

George said, "Come on Simon, let's take the weight off our feet for a short while and sit in this field under the tree," pointing to a large tree with hanging branches touching the ground.

"We had better not go there, those cows might go for us!"

"Don't be so silly, of course they won't, they are enjoying themselves grazing. It's only bulls that might charge you."

George opens the five-bar gate and tells Simon they must get the farmer's permission first.

As they make their way to the farm along a track made up with bricks and rubble, they see a large house which is painted cream, with large pink and red roses climbing the walls; the garden looked a picture. As they made their way into the farmyard, they see the farmer washing down his tractor.

George waves his walking stick in the air to get the farmer's attention; "Good afternoon Sir, I wonder if you would mind if we rested in your field?"

Pointing to a large tree in the centre of the field the farmer replies "Be my guest's, as long as you don't leave any litter about."

"Don't worry," said George, "I'll see its left as we find it; what a beautiful garden you have Sir." A big smile spread across the farmer's face.

"Yes, it has come on very well this year, but the trouble is that I cannot give the energy that I would like to put into it as the farm takes up most of my time." They both say goodbye to the farmer and make their way over to the tree. George gets his plastic mac out of his rucksack and lays it on the ground.

"This seems like a nice shady spot to sit Simon. I don't like too much sun, it gives me a bad head."

Simon gets out a large green apple from his bag and starts to peel it with his penknife.

"Grandfather, can you please tell me one of your wartime stories?"

After a slight pause, "I'll tell you a story which took place just a few years ago. It's all about a very close friend of mine after the Second World War. It was the early part of May and we were living in a little village of Burwash Weald in Sussex."

"Oh come on Granddad, get on with it."

"Who's telling the story; you or me? Or is it too gruesome for you? Now how far did I get…"

"…We were living in Burwash Weald, that's right. Well, your grandmother and I had invited your great Uncle Gerald and Aunt Kitty over for Sunday lunch."

"It was the middle of summer 1966, you were about four and staying at an auntie's house. Your father was living at the time with us at Beckside Cottage."

"I know all about that Granddad."

"Should I tell you the whole story or not?"

"Oh Grandad, please, I won't say another word."

" As you know we were living in the two-bedroom cottage down at Willingford Lane I believe it was built around the 16th century. As I said I only believe it was built in that time and there was a pretty little river about quarter of a mile down the lane."

"It was called the River Dudwell, your dad and I sat under the bridge and caught trout and eels. Yes, we had a grand time by the river; during the spring it looked a pretty picture down each side of the lane with all the spring flowers and hedgerows in bloom. I must tell you Simon, the village next door is called Burwash. Back in years past, many years ago there was a dog which came into the village and the dog's name was Burr. When the dog arrived in the village he was filthy, so they gave him a good wash. So, the villagers decided to name the village Burwash." George chuckles.

"I've been told at the top of Willingford Lane next to the park there was an old church which sank into the ground. But how true that is, I don't know; it could be an old woman's tale."

"Anyway, let's get back to the story…"

The Summer of 1966

George and all were about have a Sunday lunch of roast beef, it was his favourite, when the telephone rings. "Who the hell is that at this time of day?"

"Now now George, don't speak like that", says Jill,

He picks up the telephone, "Burwash two-seven-one, hello who is this?"

"I am sorry I can't hear you, can you please speak up."

"This is Stinky speaking, your old pal. We were stationed together at Hawkinge down near Folkestone in Kent during the Second World War."

"Stinky Jones you old devil, where have you been hiding?"

" I'm now living in the village of Wanstead, I've been moving from house to house, we just could not settle. I think we have settled down now George. Previously we were in the village of Ripe; it's halfway between Heathfield and Eastbourne."

"Well George, I was hoping to arrange a reunion of all the boys who were stationed at Hawkinge during the Second World War. Is there any chance of you coming over for a chat to chew things over? What about this afternoon George?"

" I'll have to clear it with Jill. I have to keep in her good books, if you know what I mean."

George goes through to the kitchen and calls to Jill, "Who do you think is on the telephone. It's only Stinky Jones. He would like to know if I could pop down to see him this afternoon, to arrange a reunion for all the old boys I served with at Hawkinge."

Kitty says, "I bet it will be a great old knees up."

"Bless me", remarks Jill, " that's a great surprise, where has he been hiding? I don't see why not; what about taking Gerald for the ride and leave Kitty and me to have a good old natter."

George returns the phone and Jill calls out "Don't forget to give Hilda and Stinky my love."

"Everything is okay Stinky, see you later on. By the way Stinky, is it all right if I bring a friend along?"

"Of course you can George, as I said we now live at the old Manor House, its next to the church, you can't miss it."

"That was Stinky Jones, Gerald. He would like me to pop down this afternoon. Would you like to come along for the ride?"

"That's very kind of you George."

"Think nothing of a Gerald. To tell the truth when you have gone home my life will be like hell. ' *Why have you done this, why have you done that…* ' No, I'm just joking Gerald."

"We can have a good chat on the way down to the Manor." They have just finished lunch and Kitty and Jill start to clear the table.

George picks up two wine glasses makes his way to the kitchen. Jill tells him to put the glasses down and take Gerald into the garden. "I might, I said I might, bring you both a cup of tea."

He puts his hand on his head, "If you say so dear, if you say so."

Jill tells Kitty to leave the washing up till later. "Let's get these two men out of the way first."

Jill is telling Kitty about a hat she has seen in the village shop which she had to buy.

Out in the garden George is telling Gerald all about Stinky Jones. "He has something lined up to tell me which must be very big. Stinky never does things in small measures. I said we will see him about three o'clock. Is that alright with you?"

"Just fine George."

"I should say Gerald it's about 40 minutes drive from here."

" You are sure you're happy about me coming with you to the Manor. I don't want to put you out in any way?"

"Don't be silly Gerald, it's perfectly all right by me. Gerald did you see that Jack Street has sold up and left the village? I've been told he's moved to Spain."

"That's news to me George."

"He owned the gun shop in the village and lived at the back of the shop for a great many years. I've been told he bought a flat close to the Spanish coast. As long as I can remember Gerald, he never took a day off all the years I knew him. When the shop closed he was always in the back clattering about. I bet he was worth a few bob, what do you think Gerald, he must be worth a fortune."

Kitty arrives with the cups of tea for two tired men.

They both lay back in their chairs, Kitty and Jill tell George and Gerald it's the women who deserve a lot of pampering.

"We are overworked and underpaid."

"Don't make me laugh," says George, "It's a job to get you out of bed in the morning."

"How could you tell such lies George. I'm telling you now George, when you're over Stinky's, make sure that you behave yourself. And don't let Gerald get into your bad ways either."

"I'll let Gerald look after me, is that alright?"

Kitty and Jill make their way over to the flower border. Kitty tells Jill that Gerald can go a bit over the mark.

"I'll let you into a few of his antics that he got up to in the past."

George says in a quiet voice to Gerald, "Can you here them natter natter natter. I think it's time we made a move Gerald; which car should I take the Austin or the MG?

"I think I'll take the MG for a spin. It will do it good to have a good run. These days I only take it around the village. A car like this needs a good run from time to time."

"Jill could you run Kitty home later as I don't know what time I'll be back?"

"Don't forget George you have work in the morning."

George tries to start the MG without any luck. "I'm afraid Gerald, you will have to give me a push."

After pushing the car 800 yards it finally starts.

As they get on their way George tells Gerald some of Stinky's bad habits. "It is true what Jill said. Stinky and I have had some wild times together. Stinky is like a fish out of water as far as beer is concerned. Do you know I like it this time a year Gerald, driving through the country lanes with a nice cool breeze blowing in your face."

"George how did Stinky get his name?"

"I was telling you earlier that we were both stationed at Hawkinge near Folkestone in Kent. Just a few miles up the road from Folkestone, it was the latter part of 1943."

"Whenever Stinky was off duty you would find him carving bits of wood into pipes. He carved a pipe in the shape of a bulldog and every time he lit up there was a great cloud of smoke and the smell was disgusting. I bet you any money you like he still has the same old pipe. We should be coming into Wanstead any minute now, Stinky said it was just past the church."

"Ah this looks like it and the driveway should be on the right." As George gets out of the car a black dog comes up to the gate wagging his tail, he pats him a couple of times. "I remember when Jude was just a pup; Stinky bought him from a Gypsy Traveller down in Hawkinge." They both make their way to the side of the Manor; George knocks three times.

A lady calls out in the upstairs window, "I'm just coming."

A tall, thin lady appears, very well dressed in a dark blue dress, cream cardigan and blue shoes. She opens the door very slowly.

"Hello Hilda, it's nice to see you again. You haven't changed one little bit, still the same old Hilda."

"Little bit less of the '*old*' George. I know I'm getting on a bit but don't rub it in."

"The only thing which have changed are my legs; they are not what they should be. How is Jill keeping, well, and little Simon and your son?"

"Jill is just fine and my son Frank, I wish he would find a job. Yes Simon is getting on very well and growing up fast. He is doing very well at school. He went to a school for toddlers before going to school proper."

"That is very good indeed George."

"This is a very close friend of mine, he lives in our village, Gerald Bishop."

"It's very nice to meet you Gerald; Oswald told me you were coming down this afternoon. George, just follow the path round to the front and you will see him attending to his roses. That man gets on my wick at times, he is never there when you want. No, it's all right George, it's just a joke. Could you ask Jill if she would like a day out in Tunbridge Wells, as we have a lot of catching up to do?"

"I will Hilda. I'll see you later." They arrive at the front garden.

"What did I tell you Gerald", as he points to the far end of the garden, "there he is over by the roses puffing away on his pipe."

"Stinky old pal. How goes my old Stinky?"

"Very well! Very well indeed George."

He puts his pipe into his left hand and shakes George's hand.

"Stinky, this is my close friend Gerald Bishop."

He shakes him by the hand "It's very nice to meet you Gerald. And how is Jill keeping George?"

"Just fine Stinky, just fine."

"I'll just relieve myself of these gloves and tools and then we will have a nice cup of tea over on that seat."

As he passes the front door he opens it and calls out to Hilda "Three cups of tea dear; out on the lawn."

He returns from the potting shed, "The reason why I have asked you down is I had this idea."

"What is that Stinky?"

"Hold a reunion, here at the Manor, what do you say?"

"Have you thought the cost? It will cost a great deal of money! What does Hilda think?"

"Don't worry about the cost. Hilda is all for it, I'll pay for it all."

"In some ways you must be mad Stinky!"

"No George, I been thinking very hard just lately. All those poor blighters that got killed within hours of leaving Hawkinge. In some ways, it will be paying something back to them all."

"You can count on me." says George.

"Include me in too." says Gerald.

"That's very kind of you both; thank you."

Gerald tells Stinky "Any electrical work needs doing, I'm your man."

"Over the far corner Gerald, we will have the stage and lights around the garden. I'll leave all that in your capable hands, if you need any cash just give me a shout. I'll show you where the car park will be in a few minutes. By the way, coloured lights down the driveway; I'll get some of the farm lads to give us a hand with the stage." Hilda appears with the tea with Jude walking behind her. Stinky asks Hilda to join them.

"Thank you all the same Oswald but I have one or two things to do. The trip to Tunbridge Wells, I was thinking of Tuesday next week George. Would that be alright for Jill?"

"I expect it might be Hilda. Do you mind if Kitty, Gerald's wife goes along?"

"Why not George, the three of us can have some great fun. Don't forget Tuesday next week Gerald and don't forget to tell Jill. Tell Jill that I'll confirm the time on Tuesday." Hilda makes her way back into the Manor.

Stinky tells George and Gerald that all the drinks and food will be coming from the Royal Oak. George tells Stinky of the grand idea of his.

"You love a bit of a gamble. What about clearing out the potting shed and putting in a roulette wheel?"

"I don't think it will go down very well with the ladies," say Stinky, "If you can put two strong lights in the shed Gerald, and I will get some curtains."

"All we need are a table and chairs and I'll fix the lock on the shed door, so we can have a damn good time." says Stinky.

"Come on both of you, what do you say?" Gerald asks. "You know the old saying, in for a penny in for a pound. What about having a large cake with blue and white icing, with the words something like *'The Day I'll Never Forget: Hawkinge during the Second World War'*. What part do you wish to play at the reunion George? Just lead me to the drinks table to I can keep an eye on you Stinky, and I'll help anywhere I can." says Gerald.

"Thank you Gerald", Stinky looks at his watch and shouts, "look at the bloody time."

Hilda pops her head out of the door and tells Stinky to stop swearing.

"Yes dear, yes dear" he replies.

Stinky takes the tea tray and cups inside and tells Hilda they're off to the Royal Oak, "You know we still have a great number of things to sort out. I just don't want anything to go wrong."

"It won't go wrong if you stop that swearing."

"Sorry pet. Come on you two; we are wasting good drinking time." Stinky and Gerald start to make their way to the Royal Oak while George tells Hilda to have a good time in Tunbridge Wells.

Stinky tells them both about the one and only Mrs Flyn. "She will do her utmost to find out what she can about you and any of your private business. So watch her with both eyes, I think she could be a dangerous woman."

Gerald remarks on how his legs gone stiff after sitting down. "This happens to me from time to time."

"How nasty", says George.

Stinky points to the field, "This is the one where we will have to park the cars as they arrive at the end of the driveway."

A tractor and trailer loaded with hay makes its way down past the Royal Oak.

"You can't beat the smell of fresh hay," says Gerald,

Stinky starts to reminisce "George do you remember Guy Stringfellow? If ever there was a case he was! You only had to mention the *Cat & Mustard Pot* and when he was off duty he was out of that camp like a shot. And boy could he sink a pint. The pub was only half a mile up the lane from the camp."

"What about Nicky Downs?" says George, "He would leave the pub after a pint and return an hour later with half-a-dozen rabbits. Whether he caught them by snare or whether he was well in with a poacher I never did find out."

"The pub was near forked road in a large woodland area", Stinky pauses to relight his pipe. "All the village consists of is a butchers, a post office come general store, but the most important place is the Royal Oak."

"It's bound to be," says George, "Any other shopping or car repairs we have to go to Eastbourne."

Gerald asked what the weather is like in the winter in Wanstead, "I've been told Gerald that it can be pretty nasty here. They've been cut-off for weeks, sometimes months, with snowdrifts. You have to dig your way out and that's no joke."

As they arrive at the Royal Oak Stinky opens the door and shouts "A very good evening to you Fred."

"And the same to you Stinky. How are the roses coming on, had any more luck in the local show?"

"If I win any more cups I'll have to move house to fit them all in. Just a joke Fred, perhaps after this year I might take things a little easier."

"You would be greatly missed Stinky, and I'm telling you, if it were not for you the local show would have closed down long ago. You were the only person who put your hand in your pocket and kept the show running."

"Fred I'd like you to meet a wartime buddy of mine, George Stevenson, and this is a close friend of George's, Gerald Bishop. They both live in a village not all that far from here, called Burwash Weald."

"I've been through it, but I've never stopped." Fred shakes hands with them both. "It's a very pretty village, but I've stopped three or four times at The Bell in Burwash which is right next to the church."

"That is very true," says Gerald, "The Bell is a nice little pub."

"Come on you two, the drinks are on me." says Stinky, "what's it going to be?"

"Two beers please." says George.

"Fred, I have a bit of a do coming off at the Manor in a few months time. Could you pop up to the Manor on Tuesday?"

"Any time after nine will suit me Fred."

Stinky lights up his pipe again. "Come on you two, lets make our way over to the pews in the far corner." They had only been sitting in the corner for a few minutes when Gerald passes a remark about the person sitting the other corner. "Look at that man, he keeps staring you Stinky, do you know him?"

"No, I have never set eyes on him before. But I've been told there was a new person moved into the village around three months ago, I had no idea whether it was a man or a woman. When I was standing at the bar he caught my eye Gerald and he looks a very lonely sort of chap."

Stinky calls out to Fred "Three refills in the corner please."

As Fred arrives with the drinks Stinky asked him if he has come across a gentleman in the corner before. "He's been coming into the Royal Oak for the past four weeks, but who he is I have no idea."

George asks Stinky for a list of all the people to be invited to the reunion. "If that's alright with you Stinky?"

"Yes, that's very kind of you George."

Fred collects some glasses from a table close by. "Yes Stinky, all my customers say the same thing. *He is in a world of his own*." Fred makes his way back to the bar.

Stinky takes a list from his briefcase and hands it to George.

Gerald asks if they could have the reunion on a Saturday or Sunday. "What day do you two think? We'll have to get permission from the parish council of the church."

"I would prefer Sunday myself." says George.

"Sunday would be the best day."

"Yes, I agree on Sunday", say Stinky as he starts to cough, "Lets make it the last Sunday in September and start around eight; all agreed?"

They both say, "Yes that's just fine."

Stinky tells them both that the reunion will be conducted in an orderly manner. "As I said early on that Fred will be providing all the food and drinks. I must not forget to give the Reverend Fox a call, he has only been in the village for two months and I don't know how he will react. Hilda and I are not great churchgoers."

"Don't look on the gloomy side Stinky." mutters George.

"It's alright for you to grin George, but some rectors are very funny over things like that."

"Hold on a minute you two, let me get everything down in my book. It's the last Sunday in September we should start at seven-thirty for eight and will close down around eleven-thirty."

"That's correct", says George.

Gerald gets up from his seat and says, "It's okay with me".

George takes a look at his watch. "I think it's time we started to make a move Gerald. Let's hope there are not many cars on the road tonight."

"I don't think so, not at this time of day." says Gerald.

Stinky reminds them not to forget about the one and only Mrs Flyn. "Every day she's up and down this lane on an old-fashioned bike, you can't miss her. So I've been told the Reverend Fox does not see eye to eye with her. Even though she spends quite a lot of time at the church."

George and Gerald get up from their chairs but Stinky asks them to have one more pint with him, "Come on George, be a sport. Just one more for the road."

George tells him, "Just the one and I mean one."

Stinky shouts out, "The same again Fred and a packet of my special tobacco."

"I'll be with you in just two minutes." Fred responds.

George gets up and walks to the window. "It looks like the wind is starting to blow up there is a nasty nip in the air; there was an old man just passed he was well wrapped up."

After they had all finished their pints George opens the door, "Come on Gerald, let's hit the road. We don't want to be too late back."

 Stinky asks George to stay for just one more pint.

"No no Stinky. If you had your way we would be here until kicking out time."

"So be it then George."

As they make their way back to the Manor Stinky agrees with George that there is a sharp nip in the air.

George asks Gerald, "Would you like to drive the MG home?"

"No thank you; I'm not what you call a *night driver*. Thank you all the same."

George tries to start the car without any luck. "The engine has gone cold as I don't take it out on a regular basis. She likes to play up…;"

"Aah, that's it third time lucky! Well, it's been very nice seeing you again Stinky, and all the very best to Hilda."

"The same to Jill and don't forget about Tunbridge Wells George."

"I won't Stinky."

They had only been on the road half an hour when Gerald shouts. "What the hell was that?" It was something dark and long.

"It was only an old dog fox, Gerald."

"Do you know George when you hit those brakes on I had a feeling we were going to end up in the woods."

"Not with me Gerald."

"Do you know that fox has brought back memories of an old mate of mine, we have been great friends for quite a few years, his name is Ray. Yes, that's it, Ray Mears. He lived in a cottage near Roberts Corner near Swingfield in Kent; just down the road from his cottage there was another old cottage out in the middle of the field which had three big apple trees. The apples were as big as your fist and big red and juicy. Ray went down to the old cottage late one night hoping to get a sackful. He was a person who had to nick something, that was Ray all over. But while he was up the tree, the old man came out of the cottage with his gun; he fired twice into the trees and my mate Ray fell to the ground.

And that old man never called an ambulance or the police, all he did was cover him over with a tin sheet. It was a long time later that a tradesman reported the body to the police, having discovered it after the smell, which was terrible, coming from the garden. '*I went out and shot some pigeons.*' was the only thing you could get from the old man."

"I think it's darned disgusting!" says Gerald.

"It looks like Jill has gone to bed so I had better run you home Gerald."

"That's very kind of you George."

~~~

The next morning George and Jill are having breakfast. "How was your afternoon at the Manor George, what did that urgent call entail?"

"A reunion with all the lads from RAF Hawkinge to be held at the Manor on the last Sunday in September."

"That will be nice. I'll be looking forward to letting my hair down."

"And there is another big day out."

"When is that, please tell me, when is it George?"

"Tuesday week with Hilda and Kitty, a shopping trip to Tunbridge Wells. Hilda said she will be in touch this Tuesday and let you know."

"I can tell you George I'll enjoy a trip to Tunbridge Wells. When did I last go there, it must be eighteen months or two years or was it longer than that?"

"Do you know Jill, I can't remember if Stinky told me what time the reunion would start. And I've got to get out all these important invitations."

"I'm not surprised George, knowing your head after the night before."

"What happened was this old man in the pub, kept looking at me and Stinky. When the three of us left the pub, I took a good look at him and then I said to myself, it can't be, he was killed in France. So, who he is, I just don't know. When Hilda telephones you tomorrow morning can you ask what time the reunion starts?"

"I will George, see you at five-thirty. Goodbye."

Tuesday Morning At The Manor

Stinky is speaking to the Reverend Fox on the telephone, Hilda appears.

"Oswald how much longer are you going to be on that telephone? I have not all day to wait for you. There's a great deal of work to do and I have a hair appointment later this morning. Jill will need to know what time I'm picking her up next Tuesday."

"Don't worry so much, I should not be too long, just a few more minutes. Hello, is that Reverend Fox?"

"Reverend Fox speaking."

"Reverend I wonder if it's possible for you to do me as a great favour. It's Oswald Jones from the Manor."

"If it's possible Mr Jones I would love to. I'd like to help you in any way I can."

"We are hoping in the last Sunday in September to hold a reunion at the Manor. For all the men who served with me in the Second World War at Hawkinge near Folkestone."

"What a grand idea Mr Jones."

"Reverend, I would like you to say a few words; a prayer and hymn to start the evening off."

"When did you say this will take place?"

"The last Sunday in September. It will start at seven-thirty for eight o'clock and finish the evening off around eleven-thirty."

"Oh, I'm sorry I'm pretty sure I'll be away that day Mr Jones; hold on I'll just double-check my diary. Mr Jones, I'm very sorry I was getting mixed up with August." There is a slight pause as the Reverend flicks through his diary. "Yes Mr Jones, I can confirm that day I will be free, but I must leave by eight-thirty."

"Thank you Reverend for everything."

"No Mr Jones, I must thank you for the kind invitation."

Stinky calls out a Hilda, "I've finished with the phone, it's all yours."

"Operator, can I have *Burwash two-seven-one.*"

"Hello?"

"Hello, is that you Jill? It's nice to hear your voice again."

"Before we start Hilda, can I have a quick word with Stinky?"

Hilda passes the receiver to Stinky.

"Stinky, could you please tell me what time the big event starts?"

"It starts at seven-thirty for eight o'clock."

"Sorry about that Hilda. It's been a long time since we had a good chat. The three men said on Sunday we should spend some of their money Jill! And have a good time in Tunbridge Wells." she says with glee.

"It's a very good idea Hilda. I talked it over with Kitty and she says what time suits you will suit her."

"Let's say nine o'clock at your place. Is that alright?"

"That's just fine Hilda."

"Jill what a good-looking chap that Gerald is. I can tell you now I could fall for him anytime."

"Now now Hilda, calm down. You should know better at your age!"

"Just remember Jill, you can get a very good tune out of an old fiddle." Hilda giggles mischievously

"Hilda, whatever next!"

Stinky makes way to the telephone. "Hilda, I thought you were in a hurry to have your hair done."

"Any minute now Oswald, any minute now. Sorry about that Jill, I can tell you now I'll kill that man, Oswald was trying to hurry me up. And now I've forgotten what I was saying, anyway I'm off now Jill to town to have my hair done and do the weekly shop. I'll see you next Tuesday around nine. Bye for now."

"Bye Hilda."

"Hilda I'm just going to take another look around the garden and check I've done everything correct for the reunion. I will be calling into Church Farm to see Jack Brown and ask if he will let me have some of his men to help put up the stage and anything else that needs doing. I'll probably end up at the Royal Oak. I'll see you just after one o'clock. Bye dear."

"It's good you're not driving if you're going to the Royal Oak."

"Don't worry dear, I won't get drunk."

The Trip To Tunbridge Wells

Hilda is about to get the car out of the garage, and she hears a voice calling out to her. "Mrs Jones, Mrs Jones can I speak to you?"

"Ah. It's you Mrs Flyn, good morning; how are you this morning?", and then under her breath, "who was the unlucky person this morning? What person she going to run down today?"

"I saw two men entering your drive two Sundays ago, in the afternoon, they both looked very shifty and I was not sure if you were in."

"There is no need to worry on that point Mrs Flyn. We were at home and in no way were they shifty."

"Oh, I'm sorry. I am deeply sorry Mrs Jones. The wrong word slipped out."

"So you should be Mrs Flyn, so you should be."

"I'm sorry Mrs Flyn I can't stop here talking to you. I have an urgent appointment."

"What may that be Mrs Jones? "

"Goodbye Mrs Flyn."

Jill is waiting by the kitchen window when Hilda arrives. She calls out to Kitty, "Come on let set out on a Grand Day shopping."

They all greet each other with a kiss on the cheek.

"Hilda did you want a cup of tea or coffee before you set off?"

"Thank you all the same, but I've had enough tea to make me burst."

As they enter the outskirts of Tunbridge Wells Hilda points to a turning on the right. "Just up the road is the Kent cricket ground and today Kent are playing Sussex. With a bit of luck we can watch the match after lunch. Come on what about it both of you?"

"We are both game." says Jill.

"Right, cricket it is."

As they arrive at the bottom of the road Jill tells Hilda to turn right. "See the big red building, that's the post office, we can park the car just there. If you turn the car around will be facing the right direction for the cricket match."

They all make their way up the hill to the town centre. Hilda is hurrying along in front. "Come on you two, keep up with me, this will give you both a good appetite. You'll enjoy your lunch, and the hill is not that steep." They arrive at the top of the hill .

Jill says breathlessly, "I must have a rest, as my feet are killing me." She rests for a few minutes on the steps of the Ritz Cinema. "I think Hilda, you're doing your utmost to kill me."

"Stop moaning. First up will be Woolworth, is that alright with you? Then after looking around the store we will make for the tea rooms; close-by is a store called Cheeseman's, which serve a nice cup of coffee."

"I'm with you on that." says Jill, "I'm dying for a cup."

~~~

They finished all their shopping for the morning and make their way down to the Pantiles for lunch. All three decide its got to be roast beef and Yorkshire pudding with all the trimmings.

Jill starts to tell Hilda and Kitty of the times they spent at Tunbridge Wells just after the war. "We started making regular visits to Tunbridge Wells with afternoon shopping. Then we went on for a meal followed by a trip to the cinema, to see the Bowery Boys or maybe see a show with the great Harry Mooney and Victor King."

Jill then stands up and starts to sing.

"What are you doing Jill?" Hilda gives her a stern look.

"When that old gang of mind get together, together in my hometown we were friends in the past and that friendship will last…" she croons.

Hilda gives a smile as onlookers give Jill a clap.

"What's the matter with you bursting into song like that?" Hilda whispers slightly embarrassed.

"Why not Hilda, we are here to enjoy ourselves aren't we?"

Hilda replies, "Yes, but…"

Kitty interjects, "Sit back, close your eyes and think of Christmas. Can you see all the lights and decorations, and the families going from shop to shop? And the young children looking into the shop windows looking at the dolls and toys. Toys their mothers and fathers can not afford!"

"That's quite true, says Jill " But they were all happy with what they got. It seems the older you get the spark seems to go out of Christmas, as each Christmas goes by it seems it's food & drink that matter."

Kitty says, "I must tell you what happened to us, visiting an aunt in Sevenoaks in '43.

"Do you know it's very nice at weekends in the summer we often took a trip to Burwash", says Hilda, "It's so nice to have a drive through the country lanes. I'm so sorry Kitty, that was rude of me, please go on."

"We were returning to Burwash Weald from Sevenoaks, everything was going smoothly until we came across a large number of tanks on the Frant Road, all these massive tanks each side of the road."

"We quickly stopped and parked the car and then ran across fields until we came across an oak tree and hid behind it. "

"When we first arrived there was not a soldier to be seen, but after 20 minutes an officer came to our rescue and escorted us back to the car and told us not to worry as no harm would come to us."

"Do you know there must have been at least fifty tanks each side of the road."

Hilda gets up from her chair and tells Kitty and Jill, "I'm paying the bill, this one is on me. If we are lucky we should catch the start of afternoons play. You know I would follow Kent up-and-down the country if I was on my own. County Cricket is in my blood, those are just dreams, just dreams."

Jill and Kitty insist on paying their share of the bill. They both try to push their money into Hilda's handbag, but she pulls the bag away. "I said lunch was on me and I meant it. Take your money back or I'll get very cross." They find their seats and settle down.

Kitty suggests all having a strawberry ice cream; she returns with the ice cream.

Hilda tells them both if they leave around four-thirty they could call into the nice little tearoom on the way home.

They arrive at the tearooms.

Kitty says to Jill, "What a quaint little place."

"Many people have told me about the Wishing Well and that it is worth a visit." says Kitty.

Jill asks what about poor Oswald. "Don't you worry over him; he can look after himself." chuckles Hilda.

Jill says, "Leave the bill to me this time, I'm the only one who has not paid my share."

Hilda calls, "Young lady, can we have a pot of tea for three and three large slices of your cream cake please." They are all are enjoying their tea.

"Do you know I often took a trip to Burwash", says Hilda, "wherever we were living I would go and stay at a local inn. I always went to see Tom May play for Burwash, it was a delight to watch. With Tom at the crease, it was four or six every time he received the ball; when he was playing at Paddock Wood he was the only batsmen who could hit the ball over the old church. This is back in the 1930s. You know out of his own pocket he brought part of the Kent team and the Middlesex team to play at Burwash? And what did he get in return; not even a 'thank you'. There's no give-and-take these days." says Hilda resignedly.

The Evening Of The Reunion

George, Jill, Gerald and Kitty all arrive at the Manor; George is dressed in his RAF uniform and Jill is wearing a long green dress with a cream shawl.

Gerald is an evening dress and Kitty has a long lemon dress contrasted by a black shawl.

Stinky and Hilda are at the gate to greet them and all the other guests. They all start to make their way up the drive. Stinky and Hilda will do anything for a laugh so Stinky is dressed as a ginger cat and Hilda is a long-eared rabbit!

Hilda tells George with a wink "We will be changing after the guests have arrived."

"George did you have a pleasant drive down?" asks Stinky.

"Yes thank you Stinky, there was very little traffic on the road."

Gerald shouts out "Look it's that man again, the one we saw in the Royal Oak."

"Don't worry, he is simply curious of what is going on. I expect he is just having a breather on his way to the pub." Stinky tales Gerald, "You panic too much. You know George the invitations you sent out, there was only three could not make it."

"What do you say. Not bad George . Very good indeed."

The three make their way to the Manor.

Stinky calls out to Gerald "Would you mind showing the band where the stage is?"

George reappears eating a sausage "Wasting no time George." chortles Stinky.

"I've always been a sausage and steak man Stinky."

"Too true George, too true."

"George puts his hand on the gate and says, "Touch wood Stinky, the reunion is starting off just fine."

"Let's hope it stays that way George."

Hilda had slipped away without Stinky knowing. "George, could you be a decent fellow and give Hilda a call?"

"Ah, Here at last Hilda."

"I had to get out of that rabbit suit, it was like an oven!" exclaims Hilda.

"It's the same for me, what about me having to put up with the heat?"

"Oswald, you need to lose weight."

Hilda points to Reverend Fox coming up the driveway.

Stinky calls out, "A very good evening to you Reverend Fox, welcome to the Manor. I would like to introduce you to my wife Hilda."

"Very kind of you to invite me Mr and Mrs Jones." They all shake hands. "A very good evening to you both" and he remarks that he loves Stinky's costume.

"Yes Mrs Jones, I also saw your costume of the long-eared rabbit, it was just great." The Reverend Fox give Stinky a slight pat on the head. All the guests have arrived.

Stinky, Hilda and the Reverend Fox make their way into the Manor. Reverend will you join us with a glass of sherry; a bit of the old Dutch courage if you know what I mean. The Reverend gives a slight smile and nods.

Stinky says "Now I'm ready for anything." and makes his way to the stage followed by the Reverend.

All the guests are standing in a half-circle around the stage. Stinky looks at his watch and says, "It's eight o'clock and it's time we got the show started. A very good evening ladies and gentlemen, welcome to the Manor. I am incredibly pleased to see so many old faces, and to see you all in your RAF uniforms. Let's hope you have a very enjoyable evening, eat plenty, drink plenty and be merry.

A gentleman close by shouts "That's our Stinky!"

"Ladies and gentlemen please let me introduce to you Reverend Fox from St John's Church Wanstead."

All the guests clap and cheer.

"Thank you. Thank you, that's kind of you all. I would like to start the evening off by praying for the people who suffered during the war; their injuries were big and small, seen and unseen. For all the fighter pilots who never returned and all those who were killed; let's pray for all their families wherever they may be. Now I would like everybody to join and say the Twenty Third Psalm."

Then there is a three-minute silence.

"Let us now sing *'Onward Christian Soldiers'*".

After the hymn, the Reverend finishes saying, "Ladies and gentlemen I wish to thank you all from the bottom of my heart; I wish you all a very enjoyable evening."

Stinky shouts out "Let the band strike-up with *'You Are My Sunshine'*".

Stinky and the Reverend make their way back to the Manor. "Please have another glass of sherry Reverend?"

"No thank you Mr Jones. I have to attend another appointment. If I have time I might call back later."

"Please do Reverend, please do." says Stinky jocularly.

Just as the Reverend was to leave George, Kitty and Gerald enter the Manor.

"Before you go Reverend, I'd like to introduce you to Mr and Mrs Bishop and George Stevenson."

Reverend Fox shakes hands and says "Apologies, I must dash."

Stinky makes his way back to the lawns where Hilda and Jill are talking to guests, but he has second thoughts and makes his way over to the buffet close to the Manor.

Then in the corner of his eye he notices a car in the driveway; he makes his way over to investigate. The driver of the car switches off the lights, as Stinky gets closer to the car the front passenger's window is wound down. A voice in the car tells him to get in, but after a heated few minutes he tells the person to 'go to Hell' and then walks off.

He starts shouting that nobody is going to upset his reunion, "Get lost!" The person the in the car tells him, "I will be back in half an hour. If you know what's best you just make sure you are here." The person drives off and Stinky starts to make his way back to the reunion.

He then knocks back two large whiskeys and thinks very hard; *That voice, where have I heard it before and who the hell was it?* He walks back over to where the car was standing and starts to light up his pipe.

On the steps of the Manor George is sitting with a glass of beer in his hand. Gerald appears on the scene asking if he had seen Stinky in the last half an hour. "Last I saw of him was knocking back two large whiskeys. Didn't you tell me of some party pieces he does, is that correct?"

"Yes, he plays the banjo."

"Come on, let's find him." says Gerald, "You make your way over to the stage, meet me back here in ten minutes, and I will look in this direction."

When they meet back on the front steps of the Manor George suggests he should check the Manor over.

"Only a few minutes had passed when Gerald comes running into the Manor. "I found him. I found him; he was just walking up the driveway." George and Gerald grab Stinky by the arms and force him onto the stage.

Gerald hands him the banjo and George tells him, "Come on play that banjo Stinky."

He tells them both to get their hands off. "The first thing is, I'm not Stinky. And the second thing is I've never played banjo in my life."

"I'm Stinky's twin brother, Bill Jones. Stinky has told me about you two."

"I'm George Stevenson and this is a friend of mine, Gerald Bishop." Says a slightly shocked George.

"A friend of Stinky's is a friend of mine.", and they shake hands. "He gave me a call the other day and said he was holding some shindig and would I like to come along. Stinky and I had our own farm in Kent before he joined up. Where is the old fool, drunk as a skunk in the potting shed?"

"We just don't know Bill. Not one person set their eyes on him since we last saw him when he was knocking back two large whiskeys."

"That's our Stinky!"

Bill suggests George goes to the Manor to ask Hilda if she has seen Stinky. But not a word about him being missing. "We don't want her getting upset, if he is asleep in some part of the grounds."

"Quite right", says Gerald, "quite right."

Bill decided to tag along. "Hilda my gal how we then?"

"It's nice to see you Bill. Oswald never said you were coming."

"I did not know myself until the very last minute. You know what I'm like."

"I'm afraid I do Bill. You will have to see if you can find a good wife; time you settled down."

"Too late for me. I missed the boat a long time ago." laughs Bill.

"If you don't find one Bill, I'll find one for you. Bill go and get yourself some food & drink; there is plenty of it." As Bill is helping himself the car reappears in the driveway.

Bill goes over to see what the person wants. The driver of the car shouts at him, "Well have you decided whether you are coming not?"

Bill says "I don't know what the hell you're talking about. What is it you want to know?"

"Don't play games with me. Just get in the car and shut up."

Searches for Stinky are still ongoing without any luck. George asks Gerald if he has told Hilda yet about what is going on. "Not a word George. I think its time we told her. We can't keep back what is happening."

Hilda is deeply shocked to hear that Oswald has disappeared.

"It's so unlike him to run off like this."

Hilda keeps it quiet for the time being from the guests.

"You know Hilda, its a job to tell Stinky and Bill apart if it was not for his hair."

"It is a little darker grey than Stinky's; otherwise you could not tell them apart, that is true George."

"Just think Hilda, all these years you could have been living with the wrong man. Only a joke Hilda, only a joke!"

Hilda asks George to find Bill and says, "We will see you back in the Manor, and Gerald can you make your way down to the Royal Oak see if they are both there. Also, George can you call into the rectory, he might be there and also have a quick word with Jill and Kitty to let them know what is going on."

George takes the ladies to one side and lets them into the bad news concerning Stinky. Then Kitty and Jill carry on talking to Guy Stringfellow and Nicky Downes. Guy is telling them both of the trip to Hawkinge to see the old airfield, "All the buildings have taken a good battering." Nicky had taken a walk around the old buildings and I was sitting on a large rock looking over Sugarloaf Hill, and then all the memories of the war came rushing back."

"There was Kipper May who was mad on fishing, told me when the war was over; he wanted to buy a cottage by the sea."

"Now there was Dogend Charlie, he was a case. Anything laying on the ground he would pick it up. We were all sitting on the grass close to the mess hut one sunny afternoon. Kipper was bragging to Dogend and the others they would be taking on all comers in the camp next Friday night at eight o'clock. *'I can tell you now that nobody stands an earthly chance with my golden arrows.'* he bragged."

"*'It might not take place.'* says Dogend *'Because Kipper, your head will get so big we'll never get your head through the door.'*"

"*'Hahaha, Get lost Dogend.'* retorted Kipper"

"The big tragedy was that Kipper and Dogend took off on the Thursday night and never returned. As I looked up again at Sugarloaf Hill I saw a great number of villagers bearing three crosses up to the top of the hill. And then I remembered it was Easter week and I just sat and cried. You may think I'm very silly."

"Of course not," said Kitty, "shows you have feelings for them."

Guy's eyes start to water.

Kitty takes Guy into the Manor and gives him a brandy.

~~~

Gerald arrives at the Royal Oak.

"Fred have you seen Stinky and his brother in the last half an hour?"

"Not a sight of him Gerald. Has he gone walkabout?"'"

He was due on stage with his banjo a good half-hour ago. Then his twin brother turns up and now we don't know where he has gone either."

"Having quite a night of it Gerald."

"Quite right Fred. A right old night."

I'm afraid I can't help you there as I've never met the man, his brother that is."

"Fred the only way to tell them apart is Bill has darker grey hair than Stinky."

"Perhaps Stinky has found a quiet place to have a nap. It won't be the first time he's done that." Fred guffaws. "Anyway I'll be coming up to the Manor in a few minutes. I must put a note behind the bar before I go."

"Not a word of him missing Fred. Not until we have informed the police. George is about to do that when I return to the Manor. See you later Fred."

As Gerald makes his way back a strange looking lady walks past and calls out "Good evening."

"Good evening", Gerald replies and asks, "Do I know you from somewhere, have we met before?"

The lady says, "It's Mr Bishop if I'm correct."

He asked her again, "Who am I speaking to?"

She says very quickly, "The name is Flyn, Mrs Flyn. I live next door to the church. I heard a great deal about you Mr Bishop."

"I hope it's all very good." he replies. She gives a slight grin.

"I'm on my way to the church to clean the brass and get everything ready for Reverend Fox for early morning Sunday service."

"Mrs Flyn have you seen Mr Jones on your travels?"

"Yes, I saw him around seven. Let me think now; was it seven, no it was later. I could not say what the time was, but he was talking to a man in a black car. But what they were talking about, I have no idea. Is there something wrong Mr Bishop?"

"No there is nothing wrong Mrs Flyn. I expect Mr Jones has just taken a walk."

"Yes, I expect he has." she replies.

Gerald looks down at Mrs Flyn's legs only to see them covered in mud; her shoes too, he thinks very hard. *'Why should a woman, with legs and shoes covered in mud, go straight to the church? It does not make sense at this time of the evening or is she on her way home?* But he forgets all about Mrs Flyn and returns to the Manor.

When he arrives back at the Manor George is going frantic. "What's the matter George?"

"Its the disappearance of Stinky, it's driving me around the twist. Did you see him down at the Royal Oak Gerald?"

"Not a sausage George."

"How can a person disappear in a small village. I just don't know, it just does not make sense." says Gerald. "By the way George, I have just remembered, I bumped into Mrs Flyn just now."

"That's the last old bag on my mind at the moment." says George.

"Just hear me out George."

"Well go on Gerald, lets have it. What has she been up to now?"

"That could be the big question. As I left the Royal Oak I bumped into Mrs Flyn. I asked if she had seen Stinky."

"Yes, go on Gerald." says George impatiently.

"First, she said she saw Stinky around seven o'clock. Then she said it was much later and he was speaking to a man in a black car. Who was this man and where did he come from?"

"Come with me a minute George. Look up the driveway to those dark sheds, there is no light whatsoever. Now take a look from the entrance. Are you telling me that you could tell who was in the car?"

"All I can say she must have bloody good eyes to say whether it was a man or a woman in the car. I see your point Gerald."

"George, I think she was caught on the hop and she said the first thing that came into her head. I think she is telling a whole load of lies George."

"Maybe Gerald, maybe."

"What connection did he have with the man? That is what I would like to know George. Who was that person in the driveway and what did he want from Stinky?"

"I just wonder if our dear Mrs Flyn is telling the truth. Come on Gerald, let's go and find the others in the Manor."

~~~

"Hilda I think it's time the police were brought in, what do you think?"

"Yes, we all agree." says Kitty.

I'm sorry to say this Hilda, but he could be laying in a ditch even in the lanes." says Jill.

"It's so strange he should walk off like that," Hilda asks , "Have you caught up with Bill yet?

"No. I've looked all round the lawns and there is no sight of him. I should give him another hour as he's a bit like Oswald, he liked his drink." says George.

"I'll leave it to you Hilda."

As George makes towards the telephone he spots Fred arrive. "Come in. Any sight of the terrible twins?" he asks Fred, "any luck at your end, has anybody had any sight of him?"

"They both seem to have gone into thin air George."

George dials 999. "Hello, is that Lewes Police Station?"

"Lewes Police, Sergeant Moore speaking. How can I help you Sir?"

"I would like to report a missing person."

"Could you please give me his name Sir, his age and a description of the missing person."

"His name is Oswald Jones of the Manor Wanstead and is aged around 64. His height is around 5'4" – 5'6", and he has receding grey hair. Is a little on the large size and weighs around 14 stone."

"What time did he go missing Sir?

"His car is still in the garage and it was around ten past eight. We have all hunted high and low, but there is no trace of him. There's a big reunion taking place here this evening which he arranged."

"Yes, he did tell us about the reunion at the Manor Sir."

"Mr Jones would not arrange a reunion for all of his friends in the RAF and then desert them all. Not unless he had a screw loose, in no way was he like that Sergeant."

"I'm quite sure you are correct sir. We'll have someone sent out right away. Could I have your name please."

"My name is George Stevenson I'm a great friend of Mr and Mrs Jones." "George tells the others that the police are on their way."

In the meantime, out on the lawn randy Stewart is trying to talk his wife into taking a walk behind the Manor where there is an old barn close-by. When Stewart arrives at the back of the barn he could not believe his luck. There standing in the barn was an old Sunbeam Talbot and right next to the car was a 40-seater coach in blue-and-white livery with the name JD Everet, Atterby, North Lincolnshire. "It's my lucky day", says Stewart, "come on Betty let's have a bit of slap and tickle. Bit more tickle, than slap dear; what do you say?

"I'm game if you know what the saying is Stewart. What is that dear? Strike while the iron is hot Stewart."

As Stewart opens the rear door of the car they both fall to the ground.

A man jumps out of the car and runs away down across the fields. They pick themselves up and hurry back to the Manor. Stewart shouts for George, "There was a man in the car, the Sunbeam Talbot which is in the barn."

George tells Stewart to calm down. Stewart says, "Where is Stinky, where is Stinky? I must see him now."

"The thing is Stewart, we don't know where Stinky is."

Betty jumps up from the armchair. "He's killed him, he's killed Stinky!"

"What are you on about Betty? Whose killed who and what man are you talking about?"

"We were taking a walk behind the barn at the rear of the Manor minding our own business when this man jumped out the car and ran across the fields." explains Stewart.

Betty chirps in "It was very frightening."

"Calm down both of you and come and sit the other side of the room and I'll get you both a drink."

"I'm afraid Stewart and Betty I have some bad news. Oswald, and his twin brother who turned up earlier, have both gone missing. We have hunted for them both high and low and they are nowhere to be found."

Betty gasps and asks, "You think that man has killed them both?"

"We are waiting for the police to arrive."

Hilda comes into the lounge. "Any news of Oswald or Bill?"

"Not yet Hilda, the police are on their way," says George, "I'll wait for the police to arrive before I tell the guests."

"Can you take charge George? I'm going to my room." As Hilda makes her way up the stairs there is a knock on the front door. It makes Hilda shudder.

George opens the front door. Standing in the doorway is a man about 5'8" tall and about 15 stone wearing a shabby fawn raincoat and cap.

"Good evening Sir. I'm Detective Inspector Platford." He shows his ID.

"Please come in Inspector. I'm a close friend of the family, George Stevenson. I'm looking after everything as Mrs Jones has retired to her room. It was like this Inspector, everything got off to a fine start. Reverend Fox said his piece, we all sung a hymn and afterwards the band struck up '*You are my Sunshine*' and the last we saw of Oswald Jones was him talking to his wife, Hilda."

The Inspector says, "We will have a chat with Mrs Jones later on."

"I think it would be a good idea to leave the chat until tomorrow."

"Yes we can do that Mr Stevenson."

Gerald butts in "Inspector, you're not saying that Mrs Jones killed Oswald?"

"No no. I'm not saying that in any way."

"Inspector we have hunted high and low for Oswald, and now his twin brother Bill turned up and he has gone missing too. Then we have Betty and Stewart running to the Manor shouting that they'd seen a man getting out of a Sunbeam Talbot and running down across the fields."

The Inspector walks to the far end of the room and turns quickly; he looks straight at Betty and Stewart sitting on the settee. "Is that true what Mr Stevenson just told me? You saw a man getting out of the car, and tell me what were you doing around there? Perhaps it's all lies; now what happened to Mr Jones and his brother Bill."

No sir, no sir is just as I said. We were just taking a walk behind the Manor. It's just as Mr Stevenson has told you. I saw him shoot out like a bullet and he ran down across the fields."

"Can you give me a description of this man?"

"Yes Inspector." Betty starts to sob.

The Inspector hands Betty a handkerchief, "Come on miss, wipe your eyes."

"Inspector, he was around 5'6" and oldish. It was quite dark Sir, and I could not see properly." Betty starts sobbing again.

"Don't worry my dear, we will soon catch him. What is his age forty, sixty or older?"

"I should say in his late sixties to early seventies Inspector."

"Did you get a proper look at the old man?"

"Not a proper look Inspector." Betty starts to cry again.

"Don't worry we will have him soon. Mr Stevenson can you take her into another room. Also, may I use your phone? I just need to give Lewes Police the description of the man and get PC James here with his dogs, he should arrive in about 20 minutes."

~~~

PC James arrives at the Manor; he asks Mr Stevenson if he and Stewart could show him the car.

"Is the car where the man was hiding?"

Stewart is walking very slowly into the barn.

George calls out to Stewart, "Come on hurry yourself, I think it's best if you show PC James what took place."

"Yes Sir that's the car, the Sunbeam Talbot."

PC James gets the dogs from the van in the driveway makes for the barn.

Stewart says, "There it is, next to the blue-and-white Everett coach."

PC James asks Stewart to stand back as he opens the rear door. It does not take more than a few minutes for the dogs to pick up the scent of the old man. They start to bark and are eager to follow the scent as PC James takes a tumble over some bricks.

He makes his way down across the fields with the dogs. As he was leaving he asks George if he can let the Inspector know what's happened.

"I will be going in the direction of Saunders Lane." He shouts back over his shoulder.

"George hurries back to the Manor with Stewart and bumps into the Inspector on his way round, who says, "It's all right George, I caught what PC James said. By the way, Mr Stevenson this is DC Row he would like to see the car and check for fingerprints."

"If anybody wants me Row, call me on the radio, I'll be in Saunders Lane."

George makes his way into the Manor and upstairs see how Hilda is and update her.

George can not believe his eyes when he comes across Hilda laying on the floor. He hurries back down the stairs and telephones for an ambulance. He calls to Stewart, "Could you please find Jill and Gerald and tell them Hilda has had a heart attack and could you or Betty wait by the gate and bring the ambulanceman through the kitchen. Will you let me know when the ambulance arrives as quick as you can?"

"Right George."

Gerald comes running into the Manor and shouts "What's the matter? What's the matter with Hilda, has she had a fall?"

"No Gerald, I told Stewart to tell you she had a heart attack. Betty has gone upstairs and is keeping an eye on her until the ambulance arrives."

"I'm just going back upstairs. Gerald can you make sure the men come through the kitchen and not around the front. We don't want the guests to find out just yet. I pray to God that she will be all right." says George.

Gerald says "So do I."

Stewart appears red-faced and says, "The ambulance has arrived."

Gerald says, "Bring them through the kitchen."

Stewart starts to get into a fluster and Gerald tells him to calm down when there are three loud knocks on the kitchen door.

Gerald opens the door and standing before him were two more ambulancemen dressed in black uniforms.

"Good evening Sir. We are from the Eastbourne Ambulance Station. Could you please direct us to the patient, Mrs Hilda Jones?"

Gerald tells them "We already have two men with her now from Lewes."

The ambulanceman says he is sorry, "There must have been a mix-up, my apologies, good night Sir."

Meanwhile George makes his way over to the window and pulls the curtains.

The first ambulanceman asks who was the first to find Hilda. "I did" replies George, "I'm George Stevenson and this is Gerald Bishop, we are close friends of Mr & Mrs Jones. Hilda was lying facedown I found her and then I turned her on her side".

"You did the right thing Mr Stevenson."

"It's been one thing after another; her husband is gone missing. His brother turned up, now he's gone missing too and now Hilda with a heart attack. We have no idea where both men have gone, and the police are out looking for them as we speak. There was an intruder in the barn, and we were trying to run a reunion, to cap it all. Will our luck change!"

"It does not seem to be your day Mr Stevenson." They put Hilda on a stretcher.

In the lounge, Gerald is walking from one side of the room to the other and muttering to himself "What the hell are they doing up there?" Then he noticed the ambulanceman making his way downstairs, Gerald speaks to the second ambulanceman, "How is Mrs Jones?"

"A good rest in hospital will do her the world of good. She just had a slight attack."

George tells the two ambulanceman he will follow them in his car. Just as George is about to leave the Inspector arrives, he asks, "Who has been taken ill Mr Stevenson?"

"It's Mrs Jones," says George, "I can't stop now, as I have to hurry to the hospital, Gerald will fill you in with everything."

The Inspector makes his way to the front of the Manor where he finds Gerald sitting on a seat with tears in his eyes. His wife, Kitty, has gone to the beer tent to get him a brandy. "Please tell me Inspector, why did this have to happen to Hilda?"

"You just can't tell what is around the corner Gerald."

"Too true Inspector, too true. Any news on Oswald Jones?"

"Not a word and we still have no word on Bill Jones or the man in the barn. I just popped back in case there was any news from this side."

Kitty returns with a brandy for Gerald who knocks it back in two gulps.

"If that does not put the sparkle back in you I don't know what will" says Kitty sweetly.

The Inspector tells them, "I'm making my way back to Saunders Lane if there is any news from this end keep me informed Mr Bishop."

"Of course Inspector."

"By the way Mr Bishop for the time being all the roads are closed off. He is still out in those fields or woodlands; we will have him in no time just you see. Anyway, I had better start making tracks. Please keep me informed on Mrs Jone's condition.".

Jill has been looking after the Constable with the mug of tea. "Right Constable get me back to Saunders Lane as quick as you can." orders the Inspector.

As they arrive in Saunders Lane the Inspector asks the Constable to switch off the lights and to move close to the hedge. "Constable you've got too close to the hedge now, I can't open the door. I'll have to get out on your side. I'm just taking a walk along the lane to see if any of the others have anything to report. Come and find me if you have any news."

"Right'o Sir".

The Inspector had not walked far when he stepped into a deep puddle. "Damn & blast!" he quietly exclaims, "now I'll have to walk around with wet socks and shoes;" He continues along the dark lane "…and there is not a thing in sight, only an old dog fox."

The Inspector jumps with fright when he hears the hoot of an owl close by. He spies DC Roberts and PC Gould smoking and chatting in the car. Inspector tells them to put the damn fags out, "Do you want to be spotted sitting here?"

"No sir, sorry sir."

"Is there anything to report Roberts?"

"Not a thing sir. It's quiet as a graveyard."

"OK I'm off back to my car. Give me a call on the radio if anything should happen."

"Right you are Sir."

The Inspector was about to get into his car when he hears the sound of dogs. "Did you hear that Constable? It sounds like the dogs are heading in this direction. Quick Constable, shift yourself and follow me along the hedgerow. Keep your eyes peeled along the lane in case they flush the man out."

As they make their way along the muddy path they came across a five-bar gate. They both stood by the gate a few minutes, then the Inspector points to another gate across the field. "Come on Constable, let's make for that far gate before PC James gets there with the dogs. We should have our man before he can make a dash for it."

Twenty minutes have passed and the Inspector starts to get worried. He says his PC in a quiet voice "Those dogs should be here by now; I wonder what the hold-up can be?" When PC James comes into view, "At last PC James. What kept you?"

"If you came across those fields and swamps you would soon find out."

"What's the state of play James, you have any sight of him?"

"The dogs lost the scent two fields back when we came to a ditch, I think he's gone by now Sir."

Inspector Platford sighs wearily, "Better call it a night James and radio in for a van to pick-up the dogs."

Next Morning in Lewes

It's eleven-thirty in the morning and the police get a call from a local dress shop about a woman was been pinching shirts, socks and other garments. The manager of the shop say she has followed her to the Bluebird Café.

Two Constables arrive outside the café and a tall well-dressed lady makes her way over to the police car. "I'm Private Detective Joan Richards and she shows her warrant card. We've been trying to get our hands on this woman for some time Constables."

The three of them make their way into the café. "There she is, third from the end on the right-hand side. The woman in the red jumper."

"If you will stay close to the door Dick, Detective Richards and I will make our move."

"Excuse me madam. Could you please tell me what you have in your bag?"

The woman responds shouting, "I'm telling you nothing."

The Constable tells her that he is taking her to Lewes Police Station.

"You have to catch me first!", she cries as she tries to make a run for it.

"Not so fast my lady, as I said I'm taking you in for questioning about the stolen articles in your bags."

As the lady gets out of the seat a man in the far corner makes a quick dash the door. In doing so, he knocks over some chairs and a table. The Constable shouts out, "Grab him Dick, grab him!

A swift body check from the Constable sees the man fall to the ground face-down. PC Simkins lifts him up from the floor.

"Are we in a bit of a hurry this morning? I think you should accompany me with this lady to the Police Station." The man just nods his head.

"Seems like you don't like the place for some reason." says Constable Simkins.

At the station, the lady and man are placed in the interview room and the Constables report back to the Sergeant to report on the two arrested.

The Sergeant tells PC Ryder, "Let's take a look at the chap in the interview room. It could be the missing man from over at Wanstead we are looking for."

PC Ryder opens the interview room door and the man is sitting with his head in his hands.

"Good morning Sir" says the Sergeant cheerfully, "I'm Sergeant Moore and I think you have something to tell me, is that correct Sir? I would like to know why you were so frightened of PC Ryder in the Bluebird Café. Please let's have the truth, the true story."

"I might just as well come clean. This is been like a leech stuck to me which won't let go. It's going to come out sooner or later." says the man despairingly.

"That is quite true Sir."

"My name is Bruce Renton and I live in a cottage in Wanstead." PC Ryder offers Bruce Renton a cigarette but Renton declines, "No thank you, I don't smoke."

"I can tell you now PC Ryder, I have done nothing wrong, honest."

"You give me your statement now and I'll pass it onto the Inspector."

"I will tell you the whole story."

"It had better be good Mr Renton, damn good. At the moment you are sinking in a deep pond and not a chance of getting out. Now let's have the truth." says the Sergeant sternly.

"Yes Sir, I will. A certain Bruce Renton was killed in the Second World War. I can tell you now I haven't done anything wrong, but my intentions were there and very strong they were. My intention was to kill Oswald Jones (Stinky) known to all at RAF Hawkinge. He lived at the Manor Wanstead, I got to hear of the reunion which was being held at the Manor house. It could not be a better place. Then I found the old car in the barn, all I had to do was wait inside it until the reunion had finished then I would strike. The reunion was going full swing, everything was going just right, could not have been better."

"I was determined to get my revenge for the way he treated my girl and myself during the War when we were at Hawkinge. Unfortunately, I fell asleep in the car until a young man and his girlfriend turned up. I opened the car door and I just ran as fast as my legs would take me."

"Am I guilty of thinking of something but doing nothing about it?" Renton asks. He continues without waiting for an answer, "As I hurried across the fields, I could hear the dogs not far away. I came across a ditch. I knew the dogs would lose the scent if I jumped in, So, I walked along the ditch for a quarter mile. Then I came across the lane which I followed through to my cottage. Are you sure you want to know everything what happened?"

"Yes, we would like to know whatever it may be Mr Renton."

"What that bastard did to me and my girlfriend. I'll tell you; it was early March 1943. I just returned from a raid over Germany when the Camp Duty Officer was called away on an urgent mission. The officer left in charge was Oswald Jones, known as 'Stinky'. We were all in the bunkhouse having a good laugh telling some jokes when Private 'Johno' Johnson came into tell me there was a very urgent telephone call for me. It was the village doctor, asking if I could go down to the village, to my girlfriends house, as she was terribly ill and that I should be by her bedside as soon as possible."

"I then went straight to see Stinky and asked for special leave, as my girlfriend was on death's door while having a child."

"He flatly refused and told me I would be going on a bombing raid shortly. We never went out that evening, it was not until 11 o'clock next evening. My girlfriend died the following day, six in the evening. Not only did I lose my girlfriend, but I also lost my son. Three days later my plane was shot down over the borders of France and Germany."

"Soon as my plane was shot down I lost contact with the rest of my crew. I lost consciousness and never came round until I woke up in a cottage three days later."

"The cottage belonged to an old French couple; they said I could hide there until the coast was clear and they would do their utmost to help me get back to England. After a month or two they said I was like a son to them. They could never have children and I can speak enough French to get by, so I decided to stick it out passing myself off as their son."

"Occasionally pieces of information filtered through from England. A news report said I was shot down on the borders of France and Spain and the pilot was killed. That was good enough for me, so I decided to play along with the information, and I changed my name to Charles Coleman. That is the name I went under in France. Many years later the old couple died and left everything to me. I sold everything and moved back to England. But I just could not get it out of my mind about Stinky Jones. If it were not for him, I would have stayed in France."

"I had a bit of luck when coming across to England. For sale was a nice little cottage in Wanstead which I grabbed with both hands, and it was straight across the road from the Manor where Stinky lived. All I had to do is just wait until the time was right Sergeant Moore."

The Sergeant gets up from his seat and leaves the interview room only to find one of his Constables sitting reading the daily newspaper. He shouts out, "What the hell you think this place is, a holiday camp? If you haven't enough work to do, I'll soon find some for you."

"Sorry Sarge."

"Is Inspector Platford back yet Constable? He said he had to pop out."

"Not yet Sarge, he said was calling into the Manor on his return."

"Right, let me know the minute he returns."

"Yes Sarge"

"Go and give Bruce Renton something to eat and drink and remember if you're short of work there is plenty in my office."

"Right'o Sarge."

The Constable calls to the Sergeant, "The Inspector is just getting out of his car."

The Sergeant makes his way to the toilet. On his return he knocks twice on the Inspector's door and walks in, "Good morning Sir."

"Good morning Sergeant. We had a hell of a night trying to track that man at Wanstead. The man who was in the old car at the Manor, but he gave us the slip."

"I know Sir. We have him in the cells, he is just having a bite to eat."

"That was a bit of luck Sergeant. But I'm afraid we're not any closer to solving the case of Oswald Jones."

"This is his statement; he admits his intention was to kill him. But it could not go through with it, he knows nothing of his disappearance at the reunion."

"Sergeant we must have missed something along the line."

"You know Bruce Renton opened up like the flowers of spring. He lives in Ivy Cottage, near the church."

"So I see in his statement. You had better let him go. I know the cottage Sergeant. So hope he does not wander off. Have you double-checked that he does live there?"

"Yes Inspector, he lives there."

"It would not hurt to make some discreet checks on him."

"I was just about to do that Sir."

"Let him go; get him out of here. I've been told Mrs Jones is making a quick recovery."

"That's good news Sir."

The Inspector notices WPC Hutton passing his office. "Hutton. Hutton could you please get me a cup of tea, my mouth is dry as a board."

"Right away Sir."

Sergeant Moore leaves the Inspector's office and WPC Hutton returns with the Inspectors tea and says, "Sir we have just received a call about a car, colour black, found in Saunders Lane."

"Sergeant, Sergeant where is that man?" shouts the Inspector. "They have found a black car in Saunders Lane. Get the fingerprint boys over there, quick as you can. Take a couple of men and follow me there."

They arrive in Saunders Lane to find two police cars and two policemen standing by the gate.

"Where is it Constable, where is the car?" demands the Inspector.

"Over there Sir." He points along the hedgerow. It's a black Hillman, registration number H KK 237."

"What's going on over there Constable?"

"They have just found a well and the covers been broken. The Fire Brigade are going to drain the well. By the way Sir, both ends of the lane are closed off."

The Inspector looks over the car and then heads for the well. He speaks to the Chief Fire Officer, "Anything to report?"

"Look here Inspector, there are marks where somebody has been dragged. They track from the car over to the well. The person dragging has small feet. We will soon know if there is somebody down there. You see there is iron ladder that runs down the inside wall."

Sergeant Moore tells Inspector, "There is one person who does not fit the bill."

"Who's that Sergeant?"

"Bruce Renton. Have you seen his plates of meat. Too big for those prints."

The firemen call out, "We've emptied the well and we have come across a body."

"Let's get it up on hard ground and take a look." Orders the Inspector, "Sergeant, can you give George Stevenson a call and ask him to come round to Saunders Lane as we just found a body. And can you call Lewes and ask them to send out a van to pick-up the body and also to collect Mr Stevenson from the Manor. Tell the rest of the team not to mention anything about today."

"No need to worry on that part Inspector."

PC Ryder comes running across the field. "Please sir."

"What is it Ryder?"

"I found a piece of cloth hanging on the hedge"

The Inspector makes his way back to the black Hillman takes another look inside and outside of the car. Sergeant Moore says that the cloth found by Ryder is from a grey raincoat.

"Look here, in the back seat, there are specks of blood. I wonder if one of the specks of blood match-up the body from the well." says the Inspector grimly. He looks around and sees Stevenson has arrived. "Mr Stevenson come and look at the body which we found in the well."

They walk over in silence.

"Do you know him?"

"Yes Inspector, I know him. It's not Stinky, its his brother, Bill." he says sombrely.

"Do you know anything about him Mr Stevenson?"

"Not a lot and I'm afraid, Hilda does not know great deal either. Its what you might call a closed-shop situation."

"I was about to make my way back to the station, but I will call into the Manor first. Is that alright with you Mr Stevenson? And I want to tell you about Bruce Renton; he is very much alive. Sergeant follow me back to the manner."

"Right you are sir."

The Sergeant parks his car close to the driveway of the Manor. As he gets out of the car he meets up with Bruce Renton who says "The couple I stayed with Sergeant, during and after the war, I'm going to write a book about them."

"Good for you Mr Renton. I hope it goes well."

"Thank you Sergeant. Those are the days I'll never forget. I'll say goodbye for now."

"Goodbye Mr Renton."

The Inspector appears. "Sergeant, can you pop back to Saunders Lane and see if the fingerprint boys found anything yet?"

As the Inspector was about to re-enter the Manor driveway he was greeted by Mrs Flyn standing on the grass verge with her bike, she calls out, "Inspector may I have a quick word with you? I'm Mrs Flyn, I live in the village, just across the road."

"Yes Mrs Flyn, but you must make it quick."

"I remember it well Inspector, the day after the reunion and I was on my way to the shops when a black car pulled up beside me. The driver put his head out of the window asked the way to Whiterington. I told him to try the post office or the local pub as they might know. He then drove off in his car but when I returned sometime later he was parked in the same place where I first saw him. He stared hard at me then drove off and that's the last I saw of him."

"Is that true Mrs Flyn?"

"Yes, of course it's true Inspector." said Mrs Flyn clearly irked.

"Did you take down the car number?"

"I'm very sorry Inspector, I did not."

"It's a case of you win some Mrs Flyn and you lose some." sighed the Inspector.

"What did you say Inspector? I did not catch what you said."

"It does not matter Mrs Flyn."

"By the way Inspector, was Mrs Jones taken into hospital the night of the reunion?"

Striding away, "Thank you Mrs Flyn. We know all about that. Time is tight Mrs Flyn, I must fly."

~~~

He knocks twice on the kitchen door and calls out, "Anybody at home?" The Inspector opens the door. Jude appears barking and the Inspector gives him a couple of pats and calls out again, "Anybody at home?"

George comes hurrying into the kitchen, "It's you Inspector. I was in the back room listening to the radio."

The Inspector gets straight to the point, "How is Mrs Jones and have you told her yet of Bill Jones's death?"

"No I have not Inspector. Its knowing when the best time is to tell her; but she is coming along just fine. We just don't know yet if there is any connection with Bill Jones or Oswald Jones in the well. I would say 'yes, Inspector. What if the killer thought Bill Jones was Oswald Jones, knocked him out with some object and dragged him into the well?"

"We know whoever it was has small feet. It was a great stroke of luck when we caught Bruce Renton, so he is out of the frame."

Gerald appears from the front garden. "I was just saying to Mr Stevenson I'm glad we caught Bruce Renton. He changed his name to Charles Coleman and stayed in France after the war, and now he lives just across the road." explains Inspector Platford.

Gerald exclaims "Would you believe it! And that's the Bruce Renton who was stationed at Hawkinge?"

"The very one Mr Bishop. His girlfriend died of some illness."

"I can't remember what went on at that time," says George, "but everybody at the camp, including myself, thought he was shot down and killed over France when he was returning from a raid over Germany."

The Inspector tells George and Gerald that he has just been speaking to Mrs Flyn. "She was telling me about a man in a black car."

George says, "Don't take any notice of her, she has bats in her head. It seems a mystery to me that there were so many people at the reunion and not one single person could give us a single clue about Oswald's disappearance."

"We still don't know whether he is alive or dead, Mr Stevenson. I have to get my men to dig much deeper and see what comes out in the daylight. By the way Mr Bishop, did you notice the raincoat Mrs Flyn was wearing, a bright orange one?"

"Are you sure Inspector? Every time I've seen her she is wearing a dark coloured raincoat. No, it was fawn; yes the colour was fawn."

"Was she. I'll have to look further into that. Mr Stevenson have you seen anybody with a torn coat?"

"I'm afraid not Inspector."

"I'm just going to have another word with Bruce Renton and I'll call in and see Mrs Flyn."

"If anybody comes to mind over the torn coat I'll let you know Inspector."

"That would be very much appreciated Mr Stevenson."

"Would you mind, Inspector, if I came with you to see Bruce Renton? I would like to take a closer look at our man."

"Please do Mr Stevenson."

~~~

Back at Lewes Police Station WPC Hutton receives a call about a body found in the old Mill. Gerald takes the message at the Manor. "Could you please tell Inspector PC Ryder and PC Dixon are on their way to the scene." requests the WPC.

Gerald makes his way over to Ivy Cottage.

The Inspector meets Gerald coming towards him, "I'm afraid, Mr Bishop that Bruce Renton is not a home."

"I'm glad I caught you both", says Gerald, "they have found another body, over at the Mill. PC Ryder and PC Dixon are on the scene right now."

"Mr Bishop can you give the Sergeant a call and tell him to follow us over to the Mill. What about you Mr Stevenson, you had better come along, you might be able to help. Perhaps we might have a little luck."

The Sergeant is walking over to the Mill with the farmer. "I understand it was you who found the body"?

"That's correct sir, I found the body, but I never touched it. This is the second tragic accident I've had in three weeks."

"What was the first accident?" quizzed the Sergeant.

"It was my young Cowman. He was chasing some cows in yonder field, you see over there where its fenced off. He went to head some of the cows off and he cut across the well, but the lid was rotten and in he went. The poor chap was only twenty-six. "

"Bert Stone is my name Sergeant."

"So this morning it was like this Sergeant. I was coming over yonder field to fetch them cows and I see some of the varmints missing, then I noticed the door of the Mill open. The door was always closed. I went inside I saw this body hanging over the side near the hopper."

"You have to go up those steps Sir" directs the Sergeant.

"I'm staying right here; you won't get me up them steps. Oh no, you won't get me up there." protests the farmer nervously.

"That's all right Mr Stone. You stay there, we will take over now if you don't mind."

The Inspector and George Stevenson arrive at the Mill. PC Dixon and Mr Stone are standing by the door. Mr Stone calls out to the Inspector, "The Sergeant is looking at the body."

PC Dixon is unable to get a word in as Mr Stone will not stop talking. The Inspector thanks Mr Stone for letting them know about the body.

"I like to help where I can Sir" says the farmer proudly.

As Inspector Platford enters the mill, he asks, "Sergeant what do we have?".

"I'm afraid it's a body of a young teenager; boy around fifteen to sixteen. It looks like an iron bar came down on him from up there." He points to where an iron bar is missing. "But we will have to see what comes out in the post-mortem."

As the Sergeant takes another look at the body the Inspector walks across to the window. "Oh no" he shouts, "not that lot. This is the last thing we need today."

"What's up Inspector?" asks George.

"It's those darned newspaper reporters coming across the field. Just as I thought, a piece of news gets out and they swarm like a load of rats." he says irritated. "Mr Stevenson, there seems to be a much bigger mystery to Mr Jones disappearance."

"So it seems Inspector."

"Sergeant you had better stay here and only give a very brief statement to the press."

"Is it true that you've found a body?" shouts the first reporter as the Inspector leaves the building..

"Have you found Mr Oswald Jones?" asks another reporter.

"Three other reporters shout out in unison, "What's the latest on Oswald Jones?"

"The only information I can give you at this time is to talk to the Sergeant. He will put you straight on anything you need to know. That is all I can say at the moment. Thank you and goodbye."

"Mr Stevenson, can I give you a lift back to the Manor?"

"No thank you Inspector. I'll walk back, it will do me good."

"By the way Mr Stevenson, how many cars entered the driveway? And did Oswald Jones' car leave the garage? Not counting the guest's cars which entered the driveway."

"There was my car and Gerald's car, the ambulance and the police cars; that was all Inspector."

"Right, thank you. I'm going back to the station at Lewes. I'll get the lads out to the Manor to check the tyre marks, then I'm off to Saunders Lane to take another look and see if we missed anything. That piece of cloth is on my mind."

"I will see you when I see you then."

~ ~ ~

Back at Lewes Police Station again the Inspector says, "Hutton I want you to come with me to Saunders Lane. I want to go over the ground from the well to where the car was. Also get DC Huggett check out the tyre marks in the driveway at the Manor to see if there is any match."

Later...

"Hutton pull over the side we will wait here for a few minutes." instructs the Inspector, "I want to give Mr Stevenson time to get back to the Manor. Let's hope he will come with us."

A few minutes later they arrive in the driveway of the Manor. The Inspector gets out and knocks the door and calls out, "Are you in Mr Stevenson?" who suddenly appears from the kitchen.

"I was just giving Jude his food."

The Inspector asks, "Could you do me a favour?"

"What's that Inspector?"

"If you could come with me to Saunders Lane, I know there will be reporters there. If you can make out we have found Oswald Jones and keep them off our backs."

"I'm tied-up for the next hour, but I could get Gerald to go in my place. I'll give him an idea of what to say."

"That's just great Mr Stevenson."

After a few minutes Gerald appears with his jacket half hanging on the shoulder; he has a quick word with George. Then he says, "Let's go Inspector." And they both get into the car.

"Has any news come through Hutton?" demands Inspector Platford as he starts the car.

"Yes Sir. The body they found at the Mill was a 15-year-old boy. His name is Mark Brown, he had a bust up with his family in the village and told friends he was making for Folkestone."

"Poor lad, he only got a few yards up the road." says Gerald mournfully. "Did they say how long he had been in the Mill?

The Inspector moves the conversation on, "Mr Bishop I want to take another look at Saunders Lane. I think we are missing something. I've arranged for PC Milson to go over; he is exceptionally good at finding things."

Milson is waiting by the gate as the Inspector arrives, "What have you for me Milson?"

"I just found this button close to the car, it's black around the outside and dark blue on the inside."

"Well done. Now we have to find the coat it belongs to and we have our man, or woman. Oh no, it's just as I thought Mr Bishop. Look Hutton, over by the well, they are just waiting to pounce," seethes the Inspector glaring at the press pack. "Mr Bishop if you start to make your way to the well and we will give you the nod went to do your piece."

Gerald walks towards the gate, staring at the ground and suddenly shouts with rage, "Who would do such an evil thing to poor Stinky Jones? They are right evil bastards out there, if I catch them, I'll kill them."

The Inspector, realising things are going wrong, walks over to Gerald and the reporters. "Gather round," he commands and tells Gerald to calm down, "You're not doing yourself any good."

Tears start to run down Gerald's face, "Gerald go and sit in the car." the Inspector whispers.

"All you reporters have your news for today, now clear off." growls the Inspector. He then heads back to the car with Hutton and talks things over.

"All the tracks are from the Hillman, but we still don't know who was driving the car. We must make sure the reporters are told as little as possible. Let's move back to the Manor."

As they arrive, the ambulance is there. George appears from across the road. "Damn and blast Inspector. They have only sent Hilda home early. I thought she would be in hospital another two days. Was there anything else you wanted Inspector?"

"No Mr Stevenson I just want to check on how the land lies with Mrs Jones today. I expect I'll see you later on." Hutton and the Inspector give a wave as they drive off.

They have taken Hilda up to her bedroom, she is told by the ambulanceman who has a very stern look, "The Hospital told you that you must rest, did you hear me? You must rest, those are strict orders. I can tell you now there will be big trouble if you don't Mrs Jones."

She says, "The doctors are nothing but a load of fuss pots. Just look at me George, I'm right as rain."

"You took the words right out of my mouth. You never know when the rains going to fall." says George looking bemused.

The ambulancemen make their way downstairs with Gerald reminding him "Don't forget what we told Mrs Jones."

"We will keep an eye on her, don't worry about that." Says Gerald. "But can you tell me, why did they let her out so early?"

The first ambulanceman replies "You had better ask Mrs Jones that question Sir. She discharged herself; it was only her wish to leave hospital. We can't be responsible for her actions."

"Of course, you're quite right. Thank you for everything you have done, goodbye."

George runs upstairs to find Kitty and Jill to Hilda "What are we going to do with you Hilda?"

Kitty and Jill look at George puzzled, "What's the matter George?" asks Jill.

"I'll tell you what's the matter. Hilda has only discharged herself from hospital. She should have been in another two days or longer."

"I prefer to be in my own home, that's where I'm glad to be." retorted a defiant Hilda.

There's a knock on the front door. "I wonder who the heavens that can be." wonders George aloud.

"You will never know if you don't answer it." says Kitty with a grin on the face.

"That's enough of your corny remarks Kitty."

~~~

"Good afternoon Mr Stevenson. I was just passing so I thought I would see how Mrs Jones is progressing in hospital."

"I'm afraid, Reverend Fox, Mrs Jones been very naughty and discharged herself from hospital. You may go up and see her and give her a piece of your mind."

"I will Mr Stevenson."

"Naughty naughty Mrs Jones. Who's been a naughty girl then?" he mildly castigates.

"Don't you start Reverend Fox."

"Mrs Jones, you know you were taken to hospital for your own good."

"I know Reverend Fox; but I don't like hospitals."

"But some things we have to grin and bear it, don't we Mrs Jones?"

After 20 minutes chat the Reverend returns downstairs and is greeted by a concerned looking George, "There is something I must tell you Reverend, concerning Mr Jones. He has disappeared, it was on the night of the reunion, just disappeared into thin air."

"This is the first I've heard of this terrible situation Mr Stevenson."

"It all happened just after you left the Manor. His twin brother turned up and now he's disappeared too."

"Let's hope you find them soon and nothing has happened to them. I've been away for a short time with a close friend of mine. The only thing I was told was that Mrs Jones had a grand time in Tunbridge Wells. How is Mrs Jones taking it?"

"We think the news of Oswald brought on the heart attack. That's why she must take it easy."

"I've been told they have arrested Charles Coleman."

"His real name is Bruce Renton, the police have let him go."

"I found him to be a very nice fellow Mr Stevenson."

"Anyway Reverend, the police at this stage say there is no connection with the case of Oswald Jones."

"I must be making tracks now Mr Stevenson. I'll pop in to see Hilda tomorrow around ten o'clock, if that's alright with you?"

"Yes that would be fine Reverend. I won't say word about you coming, because she will be in and out of the bed. Bye for now Reverend."

"Goodbye Mr Stevenson."

On the way out of the grounds Reverend Fox bumps into Mrs Flyn. "Could you please tell how Mrs Jones is progressing? Is she on the mend?"

"She is getting on very well thank you Mrs Flyn." Suddenly a police car appears travelling at great speed and Mrs Flyn falls back on her bike.

"Did you see that Reverend? That police car could have killed me. I'm going to have it out with the Inspector, you just see if I don't. I'll tell you now that policeman could have killed me."

"Now tell the truth Mrs Flyn. That car was a good four to five feet away and you only have a couple of scratches and there is no damage to your bike in any way. You are making a fuss over nothing."

Mrs Flyn makes her way back to the cottage looking very displeased.

Back at the Manor George is putting Hilda back into bed. Returning downstairs talking to Kitty and Jill. "I'll tell you now, give a 5 to 10 minutes she will be out of that bed. I tell you now I could kill her, and she keeps putting on that damn record the 'Spanish Bolero' by Ravel. Don't get me wrong, I like anything by Ravel but when it plays all day, it's just a bit too much."

"I suppose it helps take her mind off all that has happened to Oswald." says Jill.

"Yes it could be a way of blocking things from her mind," says Gerald, "let's give the doctor a call. Perhaps he can give her something to help her sleep."

Just as George is about to pick it up, the phone rings, "Hello the Manor Wanstead, George Stevenson speaking."

"Inspector Platford here from Lewes Police Station. I've been going over all the names who attended the reunion and there is one person's name we have no idea who he is or where he comes from. His name is Teddy Fenton."

"Yes Inspector, there was a Teddy Fenton at the reunion and he was stationed at Hawkinge down near Folkestone Kent. He lived outside

Folkestone in a small village called Ealham, no tell a lie or was it Swingfield? No, that's not it. Now let me see, it will come to me."

Inspector says under his breath, "I wish you would hurry up."

"It was the name of the policeman on the radio Detective Temple, that's it Paul Temple. Just after the war had ended his father and mother bought a cottage and a couple of acres at Temple Ewell on the road to Dover. Would you like me to check him out Inspector?"

"Yes please Mr Stevenson, it would help me out a great deal. I have to drive down to Rye concerning this case and I don't how long it will take me or how long I will be there. I might be gone two or three days, who knows."

"Before I go down to Temple Ewell, I'll have a chat with Bruce Renton."

"You do that Mr Stevenson."

At midday, the Inspector drives up to Rye.

George tells Gerald, Kitty and Jill what he has decided. "The Inspector has asked me to check out Teddy Fenton. We know Teddy's name was on the invitations list. Can the three of you be quite sure that Teddy Fenton was here?"

"May I just tell you something George?"

"What's that Gerald?"

"There was a telephone call just before the Inspector called. It was from Mrs Fenton, Teddy Fenton left Temple Ewell on Sunday afternoon for the reunion. But he never returned! She has informed the police and is very worried."

"This puts an entirely different light on the matter. Who's coming with me to Temple Ewell; Jill or Kitty?"

Jill tells Kitty to go with George "…as, I know how to handle Hilda."

"OK," George tells Kitty, "before we go I'm going to have a quick word with Bruce Renton. He might be able to shed some light on

Teddy. Jill can you hear that Hilda is back out of bed again putting her record on again?"

Kitty and Jill go up to Hilda and Kitty tells her to get back into bed. Jill tells Kitty, "You see what I mean. I could not leave her with you."

"I get the message loud and clear Jill."

Hilda asks, "Are you going somewhere Kitty?"

"No Hilda, Jill was saying if I had to go out."

Jill tells her firmly, "When we say *stay in bed* we mean it. If you're good, I'll bring you a nice cup of tea or coffee and a scone."

"Its just so boring laying in bed."

"What is wrong with the radio Hilda?"

"There is nothing any good on it. Could Gerald come and talk to me or could George come up."

"George has got a lot on, so just behave. I'll send Gerald up with your tea."

Kitty is packing a bag for herself for the long journey.

Jill asks Gerald if he could take Hilda a cup of tea and two scones. "…and have a chat to her for a short while; take the Daily Sketch up to her, but don't give it a her until you have finished your chat. Then perhaps we might get a little peace."

"You don't mean that Jill." says Kitty as she makes her way to the front door carrying her overnight bag.

"No I don't, but she makes me lose my rag at times."

George returns from Ivy Cottage. "Yes that's definitely Bruce Renton, I asked him some questions about the Second World War, which only he would know and all his answers were correct. He said he remembered Teddy Fenton arriving in the driveway but that's all. Are you ready Kitty, and did you see my bag Jill?"

"Your bag is on the settee."

He gets out his wallet. "Now let's me see what I need. I'll need cash, petrol, now do I need anything for the journey. If there is anything else we will have to stop on the way." he mumbles to himself.

"Come on Kitty get your togs on and let's get on our way. I think we will shoot off to Folkestone and up through Hawkinge and branch off further up the road."

~~~

As they arrive in Folkestone George points out, that on the right-hand side is the Central Railway Station.

"This is the turning on the left for Temple Ewell. Do you know Kitty, that Temple Ewell is a very pretty village? It has a large estate with a beautiful lake and woods close by, and there's a stunning waterfall to be seen. If I lived close by I would take all my walks through the estate every day."

"We are just coming into Hawkinge and the airfield is on the left; if we go up the road on the left, look that road near the Co-op." directs George. "If you go up past the camp you'll come to the pub, Cat and Mustard Pot; OK now we should soon be coming to the Black Bull on the right. Should be around ¾ mile to the right-hand fork which goes through to Temple Ewell."

"I was just thinking George, during the Second World War, you were a very dark horse, am I correct?" quizzes Kitty.

"Not true Kitty. I would not look at a woman twice."

"That's just what I mean George. The first time was enough."

"What are you trying to do; give a dog a bad name?" laughs George.

"Only joking, only joking George." giggles Kitty as they drive down the hill towards Dover.

"Over there!" shouts George. "Those big iron gates; that's the estate, you will love it when you see it Kitty. I would really like to see the estate stay as it is; if anything happens to the old lady, the last thing you want is a housing estate. It would be a great pity. Look over there Kitty, that old upright man walking his dog. He might know where Mrs Fenton lives."

Pulling over, " Excuse me sir. Could you please tell me if you know where Mrs Fenton lives?"

"Yes, it's two doors the other side of the bakery, you can't miss it. It's the only green door in the street." replies the gentleman.

As George and Kitty get out of the car George remarks on the village, "Do you know Kitty, this is a quaint old village and it has not changed one little bit. But it was a great surprise to me to hear they had moved here."

"What a beautiful place this village is." remarks Kitty as George knocks twice on the green door.

The door opens very slowly and a little white-haired lady standing in the doorway calls out, "Who's there, who's there?"

"It's George Stevenson, I served with Teddy Fenton in the war. You telephoned Oswald Jones at the Manor Wanstead and said that Teddy was missing. Is that correct?"

"That's correct." replies Mrs Fenton, "Come in, come in both of you. I've just been having a little snooze. You know I can't get to sleep at night. The nearest telephone box is down near the pub, The Crow. When I telephoned the gentleman at the Manor he told me that you were staying there, but never gave me any other details."

Yes Mrs Fenton, that was Gerald Bishop. Mrs Fenton this is Gerald's wife, Kitty."

"It's very nice to meet you my dear. George have you known Kitty and her husband Gerald very long?"

"For a great number of years Mrs Fenton. We live in the same village, Burwash Weald. Anyway never mind about us, what's all this about Teddy going missing?"

"George, please call me Rose." as she walks across the room and turns of the radio she says, "Now, first things first my dears. Before we start talking and make both a nice cup of tea and a scone. You must try my scones after that long journey, what do you say George?"

"I'll give in to that Rose."

Kitty gets up from her chair makes her way to the kitchen, "Let me give you a hand Rose."

"You will do no such thing Kitty. Get back in the other room and sit down close by the fire. There is a rocking chair with two cushions and a large ginger cat with a mixture of ginger and brown."

Rose returns with a tray of tea and some scones. "Yes George, that's Albert the ginger cat and over there in the corner is Anna on the chair. Come on you two drink your tea and have some of my specials. Now get them down you while they're still warm. Every time Teddy was on a home visit he would always return with a cake or some buns and would always share them with me."

"All I can say is that you are a dab hand at making scones." says Kitty. "Now come on Rose, sit down and let's sort out what time Teddy left and what he said before leaving home."

"Well, we went shopping in Canterbury on the Friday. We left here around ten in the morning and we must have returned around three; everything in the evening was nothing out of the ordinary. Part of the evening he had the radio on and then he settled down in his armchair with a book. It was a book on the countryside; he likes all books like that. Next morning he woke up around seven had his cup of tea and then left to get his paper. He always likes to glance through the paper over breakfast and then he reads it right through later in the morning. Our meals are exactly the same every day, lunch was at one o'clock. On the Sunday he had a bath and then dressed, had an early tea before he left for the reunion at three-thirty."

"He wanted to take his time to Wanstead, he did not want to rush. You see he promised me that he would leave the reunion around eleven. Just after you left the Royal Air Force he had this illness whenever he went into town he would suffer blackouts. This lasted two and a half years, and then suddenly stopped. Doctors could not put their fingers on the cause of the blackouts. Let's hope they have not started up again."

"It's very strange after all this time if it should start up again, he's been taking his tablets properly. It could be the case of his disappearance…" Rose's voice quietly drifts away.

"What a worrying thought." says Kitty in a soothing voice.

Rose snaps out of her thoughts and says, "Look at the time, its half past eight, time seems to fly. I must start to get you both some tea or should I call it supper?"

Gerald tells Kitty and Rose, "I'd better go make a phone call to Gerald and see what has changed over the past hours. Kitty would you like to come down for a drink at the Crow & Bottle? And I'll bring you a bottle of stout Rose."

Rose asks George to bring back four large bottles of stout. Kitty tells George, "I'll stay behind and have a natter with Rose."

~~~

A little later George returns with four large bottles of stout. Kitty calls out from the kitchen, "Did Gerald have much to say?"

"I had no luck. Every time I tried, it was engaged."

"As I was just saying to Kitty, I'm going to put some clean sheets on Teddy's bed and Kitty can sleep there tonight. George you can sleep down here by the fire, is that alright with you George?" asks Rose.

"I was thinking Rose, perhaps we should make a way back to Wanstead."

"You will do no such thing and that's an end to the matter."

"If you say so Rose."

"And I'll bring down some extra blankets in a minute just in case Teddy returns, he can sleep in the armchair. Will you be all right sleeping on the floor?"

"Just fine Rose, just fine. I slept plenty of times on the floor at Hawkinge."

"And make sure Teddy does not go into his bedroom."

A while later they sit down to their meal. "Anybody for a cup of tea?" asks Rose, "the kettle has just boiled but I was not quite sure who was having tea and who was having stout."

Kitty replies, "I'll have a glass of stout."

"And so will I." adds George.

"Right, its stout all round."

After a hearty meal and a good drink, they all retire to bed.

As Rose makes her way up the stairs she calls out to George, "George layoff that stout."

"I'm just having one more glass Rose."

"It's only what Teddy has told me about you and the beer."

"Nothing but lies Rose, nothing but lies." chortles George. "Good night all."

The Next Morning

George returns to the cottage after getting the morning paper, as he opens the door Rose is standing with her hands in the air and has tears running down her face. "George, look here my Teddy has returned."

She gives him a big hug and exclaims "Teddy, where have you been the last few days? I thought you had been killed. I am so glad you are back home!"

"So are we." says George.

"That's quite true." says Kitty with a smile on her face.

Rose says, "Come on Teddy, sit down and let's get some food down you. And afterwards you can fill us in where you have been for the last few days."

Teddy tucks into his hearty breakfast and asks, "What have you been up to George, after you left Hawkinge? Before you came to Hawkinge you were stationed at Hemswell Cliff in Lincolnshire as I recall."

"That's correct Ted."

"George, can you tell me what was going on at the Manor? There were police everywhere."

"Well, it was like this Teddy. Everything started off very well, the Rector said his piece and then Stinky went over to the bar. Myself, Jill, Kitty, Hilda and Gerald were having a drink with Stinky. By the way Teddy, Gerald and Kitty are close friends of ours. Stinky said, '*I'll be back in a minute*', and he left his glass on the table. The big mystery is that he never came back and to this day we have no idea where he could be. And as for Stewart and Betty, well you know what they are like."

"Yes I do George, those two were a nightmare at Hawkinge. She was always waiting at the camp gate for him."

"They both came across this man in a car in the old barn at the back of the Manor. Who do you think that man was Teddy? I'll tell you

Teddy; it was Bruce Renton, and his face was very badly scarred. He was out to kill Stinky over what happened at Hawkinge. Hilda had a heart attack and she was rushed into hospital and then the police found a body of a young lad who ran away from home. He was staying in a windmill when an iron bar came down on him."

"My God!"

"There's more. The farmers cowman was getting the cows in for milking when some ran astray. He went over to the well to cut them off, but the boards were rotten and he fell in. It was some hours later before they found him."

"How terrible. What a way to go."

"The reason why I came down was…"

Teddy butts in, "They don't think I killed Stinky Jones do they?"

"No Teddy, they wondered if there might be any slight clue you could give them. Is there anything you might have seen during the evening?"

"Not a thing George. Wait a minute, I did see something."

"What was that Ted?"

"A black car pulled up outside the gate of the Manor, but nobody got out. I thought it was a bit odd, then I saw Stinky speaking to the driver. But I could not see who the driver of the car was. Next thing I saw was Stinky waving his hands in a rage. Then the car left. I said to myself, '*I wonder what all that was about.*'"

"You have been a great help Teddy. I'll give the police station a ring at Lewes, let them know the news. You know Teddy, we all searched the village with the police, high and low, not a single clue was found."

"George, do you think Bruce Renton had anything to do with the case?"

"No Teddy, he might have murder on his mind, but he got cold feet. That reminds me, I must give Gerald another call."

Teddy says with a laugh, "Who's the young lady George?"

"That's my mate's wife, Kitty. We live in the same village, Burwash Weald."

"Are you telling the truth George?" Teddy asks with a slight grin. Kitty's face goes a little blush.

"Don't be so silly Teddy." admonishes Rose, "Pull yourself together!" she shouts, "…acting foolish in front of our guests."

"My apology to you both, Kitty and George." says a chastised Teddy.

~~~

Later George returns from the phone box. I have passed the message onto the police. Still no luck with Gerald. Every ruddy time I telephone the number's engaged, what's he up to?"

Teddy is now ready to explain himself.

"As I was telling the three of you early on, all I can remember is leaving the Manor around ten-thirty, as I told mum before I left that I will not be back too late. After leaving the Manor the next thing I can remember was coming to a folly at Hadlow near Tonbridge."

"What were you doing right out there?" asks George. "That is miles off the beaten track heading in the wrong direction."

"I know that now," says Teddy, "There was just no way I could let anybody know where I was. My wallet was missing with all my money."

~~~

"As its a nice morning what about coming for a walk George?" asks Kitty "Or shall we go for a quick one down at the Crow & Bottle? It would not hurt, just one or two."

George doesn't need asking twice.

"Good morning." greets the landlord.

"Good morning landlord, how are things this morning?" responds George cheerily.

"Not too bad. Yes, not too bad."

"This is my close friend Kitty Bishop. I told you about her last night."

"I hope he said all the good things about me." says Kitty.

" Good to meet you Kitty. Yes, they were all nice things. By the way, my name is Tom."

"Likewise Tom."

"How is the old lady this morning. Is there any news about Teddy?"

"Yes Tom. He turned up first thing this morning. He had been staying at the Folly near Hadlow, just the other side Tonbridge."

"Yes, I know the village it's a nice little place. Its just past Tunbridge Wells."

"That's correct Tom. I expect Rose will call in and give you the full details of what went on. As I said, she will tell you all the ins and outs of his outings."

"Whether she will or not, she will definitely be in for her stout. I've never known her to miss a day, only if she is under the weather; and that's not very often. You know George, she is 79 years old?"

"I thought she was moving up in years Tom. But at times she only looks in her late fifties."

"I hope I look like that when I'm her age." says Kitty.

"Perhaps you will." says George.

"Anyway George drink up. I think we should give Gerald another call. It's been nice speaking to you Tom." says Kitty cheerfully. "We should be leaving after midday; we might meet up again in the future."

"I hope so and all the very best you both. Remember me to Rose and Ted."

"I will Tom."

"George, that landlord is a charming person." says Kitty.

"Yes Kitty. There are some landlords, it is awfully hard for them to give a smile. Now let's see if Gerald is going to answer the phone. Damn and blast, it's still engaged!"

"Do you want to wait a few minutes longer George?"

"No that's it. They can't say I never made the effort to call them."

Back at Lewes Police Station

The Inspector has returned earlier than expected from Rye. Sergeant Moore takes a cup of tea into the Inspector. "Any luck at Rye sir?"

"Yes Sergeant, a great deal of luck. For the moment I'll be keeping it under my hat; you know what I mean," the Sergeant starts to laugh, "What's so funny Sergeant?"

"Under your hat. Never mind sir."

"Sergeant Moore was there anything you would like to discuss?" says the Inspector displaying no sense of humour whatsoever.

"No sir."

I'm sure you have plenty to get on with."

"Yes sir, right away."

Back at Rose's Cottage

"Did you get through George?"

"No such luck Rose."

Rose makes her way to the kitchen.

"We will have time for just a quick snack Rose and then will be on our way, nothing too special Rose." George tells Rose, "We did not mean that quick."

"I told you both yesterday I like to be on my own in the kitchen. Come on, out of my kitchen let me get on. What would you like Kitty, ham, cheese and pickles?"

"That will do just fine, I leave it to you."

"This food I'm doing now, is something extra to take with you, right George?" quizzes Rose.

"Right Rose."

"I know just the thing I'm going to give you both. Go sit down George, you're getting in my way."

Kitty is telling Teddy what a nice man the landlord of the Crow & Bottle is. "Yes Kitty, Tom is one of the nicest people you could hope to meet. He would help anybody and never take anything in return. There are very few people like that nowadays."

"You're quite right Teddy. Whatever you have been cooking Rose? It's a great smell, whatever it is."

Rose asks Kitty to lay the table.

Kitty says, "I'll put these warm plates on the table for you Rose."

"Come on you young varmints, sit down and get this down you" says Rose warmly, placing down plates of bacon, eggs and mushrooms together with slices of toasts and mugs of hot tea.

"You have done us proud, this will go down just fine." says George tucking in heartily.

"If this does not warm the cockles of your heart, nothing will. Would you like any more?"

"Yes please Rose." replies George between mouthfuls.

"We all know what you are George." laughs Rose.

"Yes I know. I know"

Rose returns from the kitchen carrying a large black frying pan. "There you are now George. Tuck in."

Kitty tells George. "You must have put on a good two stone."

"Don't believe it Kitty." chortles George.

"Let me help do the washing up. It's the least I can do," says Kitty, "George is talking to Teddy about the time he spent at Hawkinge."

Gerald tells Jill the word has got out about Stinky. "…All because Mrs Nosy Pants, (Mrs Flyn), has been shouting her mouth off."

"Yes, she mouthed off to all the villagers and the outskirts of the village." agrees Jill.

"I wonder what George and Kitty are having down at Temple Ewell. George should have phoned by now; I wonder what's up. Knowing George, he might have had too many beers. He probably fell asleep in the evening."

"But he's had all day Gerald."

"No I don't think that is true Jill. If he says is going to call, he will call. There must be another reason."

"Sergeant Moore, I would like to pay Mrs Flyn another visit. You come along with me and Hutton and Sergeant would you please take notes?"

"Certainly sir."

A while later…

The Sergeant gives three hard knocks on the door. A husky voice calls out "Who is there?"

"It's Detective Inspector Platford and Sergeant Moore."

The door opens very slowly.

"Yes Inspector and Sergeant, how can I help you on this fine day?"

"We are hoping you can help us with our enquiries."

"I'll do my very best," she replies, "Come in both of you and sit down. I'm sure both of you would not say no to a cup of tea."

"Thank you Mrs Flyn."

After a few minutes she returns with the tea. "You were saying Inspector, your enquiries into what?"

"If you would like tell us anything you like to get off your chest; is there anything you think you would help us? How long have you known Oswald Jones?"

"To tell you the truth Inspector…"

"I hope you are telling the truth Mrs Flyn," says the Sergeant. Mrs Flyn starts to laugh nervously, "You were saying Mrs Flyn?"

"I was about to say, I arrived two weeks before Mr Jones bought the Manor Wanstead."

The Inspector asks, "Had you ever met Mr Jones before you came to the village?"

"No, definitely not."

"Right, thank you Mrs Flyn. That will be all the time being."

As they walk back up the path and out of earshot of Mrs Flyn, the Sergeant says "She is lying through her teeth Inspector. You see her face when I said about telling the truth?"

"Yes Sergeant, I saw it. That's why I decided to let her stew for a little longer. It will do her good."

"I can tell you Sir, she knows a great deal more than she is letting on. Let's give her another grilling in the morning."

During this time George and Kitty have arrived back at the Manor. Gerald has a go at George not phoning while he was away. "I would call you if you got that damn phone. Same thing over and over again. It was the same thing this morning, always engaged." Retorted George

"I'm very sorry George."

Meanwhile the Inspector says, "Lets see if there is any news at the Manor. Drive down to the entrance Hutton, we will walk the rest."

"Right'o Sir."

As the Inspector and Sergeant make their way up the drive Gerald is giving Jude his meal by the back door. "Good afternoon Mr Bishop."

"Good afternoon Inspector, Sergeant."

"We have just been having a chat with our Mrs Flyn."

"A very strange woman," says Gerald, "I can't remember at the moment if I told you about the night of the reunion. When I bumped into Mrs Flyn as I was leaving the Royal Oak she had been on her travels in mud, her knees and shoes were covered in mud. That was the night *before* we had the big downpour of rain. It looked like she had tried to clean some of the mud off her legs. We exchanged a few words and she said she was making her way to the church; she said she had to get things ready for the Sunday service. But when I saw her, it was Sunday evening and she said she was about to drop off a magazine to a Mrs Williams. That was about eight-thirty in the evening. I tell you, that woman is very strange. And it was a very strange thing to say at that time of the evening."

"Yes Mr Bishop it was a very strange thing to say. Did you get all that down Sergeant?"

"I did Inspector."

"Mr Bishop on my trip to Rye I found out a great deal about Mrs Flyn. We should know all the truth within the next twenty-four hours."

George tells the Inspector, "Things were not quite so bad as we thought. Teddy turned up none the worse for wear. He only ended up in the May's Folly in Hadlow near Tonbridge."

"How did he come to get there Mr Stevenson?"

"To tell you the truth Inspector, I never got the full story from him. You know it was a great shock to Rose and Teddy that Stinky is missing."

"As I was telling Mr Bishop we should have this case cut and dried sometime in the next twenty-four hours. I think its time we made a move Sergeant."

George thanks the Inspector for everything.

Gerald calls out to Jill and George, "You both like a cup of tea?"

"Could you please give Kitty a call, she's gone upstairs George."

Five minutes later all sitting down with cups of tea, George says with a laugh, "When I tried to telephone you I thought you were both away on holiday."

Jill grabs Kitty's hand and takes her to the kitchen. "Now you can tell me every little detail of what went on." George appears, Kitty asked him to tell Jill and Gerald what went on.

Kitty says, "There is not a great deal to tell. Come on George tell them."

"After he left the Air Force in Hawkinge, Teddy started having fainting attacks. They lasted around two years and suddenly it stopped.

Everything was okay for two years then it came back to haunt him. It cleared for two years and now is back again and the hospital cannot put their finger on the cause. He left the reunion on the Sunday night and had another attack."

"Hold on a minute, the kettle's boiling. Let's have another cup of tea."

Gerald returns with the tea. "You were saying George?"

"Yes, you ought to meet old Rose. She's a grand old stick and if anybody can give you a good old fry-up she can and at the age of seventy-nine she still walks down to the pub for her glass of stout."

Gerald says, "She must be a grand old lady."

"She is definitely that Gerald."

Kitty and Jill make their way into the lounge and Gerald follows them in with yet another tray of tea.

"Not more tea Gerald, I'll burst." says Jill.

George asks the ladies, "What lies of you been saying about me?"

"I haven't said a word, only about that blonde in the Crow & Bottle at Temple Ewell." giggles Kitty.

"What blonde? I haven't seen any blonde!" exclaims George reddening.

"Does not take much to get you hot under the collar." says Kitty continuing to delight in George's discomfort.

George changes the subject and asks what has been going on this end.

"Well, the one and only Mrs Flyn has been all around the village ranting on about Stinky." says Jill.

There is a loud knock at the front door.

Kitty opens the door and shrieks with joy. "I cannot believe it, its Stinky!"

"Come in quickly Stinky. George closes the curtains. Gerald call the police right away and tell the Inspector." orders Jill in a rush. "George lock the front door."

"Where have you been all this time Stinky?" asks George, somewhat in shock.

"I tell you the truth that I have no idea what happened to me. From the minute I left here I just can't remember one little thing. I never came too till sometime later in your garden shed at Burwash Weald. But the strange thing is I have never, I repeat *never*, been to your cottage of Burwash Weald before."

"I tried four times to phone you that without any luck, the only thing I can remember at the Manor was a large black car. It was in the driveway and I remember going to see who it was."

"Come on Stinky," says Gerald impatiently, "out with it, who was in the car? Did you know the person who was driving the car?"

"Yes Gerald, I know who was driving the car; but its for the Inspector's ears only. The person drove off and shouted to me '*I'll be back in half an hour, make sure you are here.*'"

"Just after the car left I slipped and knocked my head and my mind went blank."

George tells Stinky he has bad news, "Concerning your twin brother, Bill…"

It hits Stinky hard and he shouts out. "My brother Bill, where is he?"

"I'm afraid, Stinky he is dead. I'm so sorry."

George continues, "Bill turned up at the reunion and he was the life and soul of the party."

"That's Bill all over; he likes a good time." interjects Stinky mournfully.

"But when that black car turned up he must have gone into the car and the car drove off. The next thing we knew the police found him in a field, down a well off Sandfield Lane. As I said, he was dead as a door nail." says George somewhat insensitively and Jill shoots him a dirty look.

The Inspector arrives and knocks on the front door. Gerald opens the door.

"Inspector we have some very good news for you."

"I could do with some good news Mr Stevenson."

"Yes Inspector we have Oswald Jones here." Gerald says excitedly. "Please come in. Our dear friend Stinky has turned up. Wherever he has been or anything to do with the case will have to wait. He needs to rest."

"But Mr Stevenson he can't stay here because he's the vital part of the case. I know just the place he can stay. I'll bring the car round to the front door; we will put him in the back seat and cover him with a blanket. Could you please get one for me?" The Inspector looks George in the eye and says, "Not a word to Hilda or anyone else."

"Your secret is safe with me Inspector." assures George.

"You see Mr Stevenson, the whole case is coming to a head now."

"I quite understand Inspector. I'll see you when I see you Inspector, goodbye."

"Goodbye Mr Stevenson."

There's a knock on the door again. "It must be the Inspector again." says George as he opens the door, "Oh, it's you nurse, good afternoon."

"Good afternoon Mr Stevenson. You seem a little surprised to see me."

"Don't worry about it nurse, I'm in a bit of a daze. The other three are upstairs with Hilda."

She arrives upstairs. "I'm Nurse Hunnisett, good afternoon to you all. I'm here to see Hilda, hope I picked a good day with you Hilda. I understand that you had a bit of an upset with Nurse Harding, is that true Hilda?"

"Perhaps I did get a little hot under the collar."

Kitty remarks, "She is like a bear with a sore head."

"Thank you very much Kitty." says a glowering Hilda

"It's true Hilda and you can't disagree with me."

"We are not saying nothing." say Gerald and Jill.

"That's you all done. You're now fit to meet a king." says Nurse Hunnisett, "There are two things I must remind you. Don't get out of bed and don't make your bed untidy, do you understand?"

The nurse comes downstairs, "Hilda is getting on just fine. She's just like you said, hot-headed. Goodbye for now everyone."

"Goodbye Nurse Hunnisett."

Suddenly Kitty rushes into the lounge shouting, "I don't care a damn what the three of you think... I'm sticking with Bruce Renton, there must be a number of secrets he is hiding."

"Come on Kitty. Give me three good reasons why it could be Bruce Renton."

"No, you give me one good reason why it should not be him." she shouts back.

"You first Kitty."

"He has already admitted his intention was to kill Stinky".

Jill asks, "Why would Bruce want to kill Bill Jones? He did not know him or even meet him."

"The reason was, Jill, Bruce Renton slipped up and killed Bill Jones thinking it was Stinky."

Gerald asks Kitty "What time was it when he was in the barn?"

"Around eight to eight-thirty."

"That was about the time Betty and Stewart saw him getting out of the car. They both told us he jumped out of the car and ran down across the fields."

"How many miles to Saunders Lane? Come on Kitty tell me."

"I don't know, I have no idea."

"I can tell you, it is two and a half to three miles. So, did he hurry back across the field and hunt for a car? No Kitty, it's just not on."

"Alright Gerald, I take your point."

"Did they find any prints on the car?" asks Gerald.

"I have no idea," says George, "they seem to be keeping us in the dark."

"I would like to know what went on in Rye," says Gerald, "the Inspector had a very short interview with Mrs Flyn, so the Sergeant said. As I said before that woman is a very dark horse."

Following Day At The Manor

The telephone rings, "Hello, the Manor Wanstead, George Stevenson speaking. Oh, it's you Inspector, how can I help you?"

"We have been in touch with everybody concerned with the case. If it's all right with Mrs Jones we would like to hold a meeting at the Manor? At around 2 o'clock."

"That will be fine Inspector. Yes I think so, yes, that will be all right."

"Please make sure everybody at your end attends Mr Stevenson."

"By the way Inspector, Teddy and Rose Fenton from Temple Ewell will be here."

"I must be losing my head Mr Stevenson. The meeting is the day after tomorrow. Sorry about that."

George calls out to Kitty, Jill and Gerald. Gerald pokes his head around the kitchen door "What's the matter George?"

"That was the Inspector on the phone we have to have an early lunch the day after tomorrow. Because he will be holding a special meeting here at two o'clock; every suspect will be here in the lounge. Hilda must attend the first part of the meeting."

"Just you wait and see, the fireworks will fly, I can feel it in my bones. You mark my words." says Kitty.

"I must call Rose and Teddy Fenton to tell them what time to arrive and tell them to bring the landlord of the Crow & Bottle."

Two Days Later At The Manor

It's one o'clock at the Manor; starting to gather outside the gate are reporters from all around the country.

First to arrive as the Inspector followed by Sergeant Moore with four police Constables following close behind.

Next to arrive is Bruce Renton, the farmer and Mrs Flyn. Then comes Simon and Betty, Rose and Teddy Fenton and the landlord of the Crow & Bottle and then the landlord of the Royal Oak.

Everybody has gathered in the lounge. The Inspector walks over to the lounge door and locks it and stations the Constables in front.

"Now Ladies and Gentlemen I have all your names down in my black book, so all of you sit down and listen to what I have to say. We start off with Oswald Jones's wife, Hilda. I'm sorry about this Mrs Jones."

She gives a slight smile. The landlord of the Royal Oak asks, "Can somebody tell me what motive she had for getting rid of her husband?"

"The time she could not account for movements was very short indeed and it was definitely no false alarm, her heart attack. So, I think we can say she is a non-starter." concludes the Inspector.

"Thank you Fred for those comments."

"Mr and Mrs Bishop did not know Oswald or Hilda Jones until Mr Stevenson brought him to the Manor some weeks before the reunion, and I can rule out Mr and Mrs Stevenson as they have been great friends from the time he left Hawkinge."

"Bruce Renton had a very strong grudge against Oswald (Stinky) Jones, for the loss of his girlfriend and his child."

"But as time passed Bruce put all the sadness behind him. In fact, he said 'Whatever happens in the future nothing will ever bring them back.' And I'm afraid Simon and Betty are nonstarters the only thing on their mind is sex and you will never change them. But now I would like to tell you a story of a young boy."

Everyone listens with rapt attention.

"This boy was not a very bright child; he was always at the bottom of his class at school. When he was at home, anything he wanted he got. To tell the truth this child was a spoilt brat, he mixed with all the ruffians around. Every year a fair came to the village. It gave him and his mates a great time; stealing bike lamps and money, anything they could get their hands on."

Oh yes Ladies and Gentlemen, there is plenty more to come, I have not scratched the surface yet. He stole 20 boxes of apples from a farmer close by. They were stolen while the farmer was in the local market. But this was only the start of how this boy would turn out in the future."

"He moved on to live with his great aunt who thought he was a lovely boy who could do no wrong. And she had quite a lot of money hidden away. The child's mother knew only too well how wealthy the aunt was. It was her plan to get hold of every penny she had; the old sob story poured out whenever they both needed cash. But the old aunt started to get very wise to their antics and she got in touch with a relation living in Folkestone. She wrote to them that her intentions were to change her will as she had lost trust in her great-nephew and could they come over to see her as soon as possible. But she did a very silly thing as her great-nephew found out her intentions. The very next day he told her he had to go to London to sort something out which was very urgent; but this was a pack of lies."

"Every afternoon, after lunch, the aunt had a long rest in her armchair and it was extremely hard to wake her. As soon as she dozed off, he crept back to the cottage grabbed a pillow and held it over her face until she was dead. He then returned to London. On his later return to the cottage the police were on the scene. He asked what was going on, what had happened? The police Inspector asked him, '*Are you related to the lady of the house?*'"

"'*Yes, she is my great aunt.*' The nephew replied." The police informed him that a neighbour found his aunt dead in her armchair. Then the show started; tears started to run down his face and he said what a wonderful aunt she was to him. That he thought the world of her and, '*I was always there to help her*'."

"Ladies and gentlemen, the depth of this case has a long way to go." the Inspector said to the assembled group sitting in dumbstruck silence.

"It did not take very long for him to get back into his usual stride. He started work for R J Sinners in Crawley, Sussex. When he was 21, the company sent him to Madrid in Spain where it had moved part of its operations. As soon as he arrived he set about making himself some quick money. And so it was not long before the conspiracy started. RJ Sinners dealt in all types of clothes which were delivered to all the top shops in England and the managers decided that Alan was the best person for the job. It was not long before Alan met up with Mr X."

" This Mr X told him to stick with him and he would live in luxury. He was dealing with goods worth anything from £70,000 upwards, the sky was the limit. This case was only uncovered after a big mistake by Alan in a café back home. He was bragging to his mates, '*This is a chance to prove myself, to show you all how clever I am. I have deposited money in Jersey, Isle of Man and a Swiss bank.*' But sitting just behind him in the café was one of the staff from RJ Sinners. He reported everything which was said back to his boss in Crawley and a full statement was made to the fraud squad. They knew if they could catch Alan in the act they would be halfway there: the whole case had to be hush-hush so they didn't frighten Mr X away. You see RJ Sinners were suppliers to many large stores in England."

"Mr X and Alan got in touch with a firm in Taiwan to make the same clothes all they had to do was change the labels, repack them and send them off to Crawley in a container; all the containers went by ship. Mr X and Alan would pick out the best garments themselves and replace them with garments from Taiwan. The clothes they kept, they sold on the black market and made a great deal of cash. Do you know to this day Alan never changed his ways in any shape or form."

"To cut a long story short, Alan got five years and Mr X got three years. If I had my way I would have given them both twenty years at least. Put them out of harms way. I would like anybody here this afternoon to tell me who is the cold-blooded killer sitting in this room."

Mrs Flyn jumps up from her chair, "I know who the killer is!" she says excitedly.

"Please tell me Mrs Flyn."

"I've said it all along, it was that Bruce Renton." she blurts out.

"You have got it all wrong Mrs Flyn. I put my last penny on it. Yes, Mrs Flyn you are a loser." the Inspector says coolly. "Because it was you, you are the cold-blooded killer. It was you who parked your car in the driveway on the evening of the reunion, between eight and eight-thirty. Am I correct?" he demands.

The blood drains from Mrs Flyn's face and she stares at the carpet.

The Inspector continues, "The day you moved here, you let people in the village think you could not drive. That night you had a few words with Oswald Jones, '*I will return in half an hour.*' Those the word you said, that is true is it not Mrs Flyn? On your return, there was a big surprise to come. It was not Oswald Jones you had in the car, it was his twin brother, Bill Jones. It did not matter how much Bill Jones told you he was Oswald's twin, you would not believe him. In no time at all you were in Sandfield Lane and you hit him on the head with a spanner. Then you dragged the body over to the well and pushed him in. I must say you are an extraordinarily strong woman; you then left the car in the field and wiped any prints off the car. Then you make your way home; but on your way you bumped into Gerald Bishop. You forgot what day it was, you thought it was Saturday. We have a very strong case against you Mrs Flyn."

"Just prove it Inspector, just prove it." sneers Mrs Flyn briefly regaining her composure.

"Mrs Flyn I think there is a person who you would like to meet."

"There is no one I want to meet Inspector."

The Inspector calls out, "Come in Oswald Jones. Could you please spare a minute Sergeant Moore and take Mrs Stevenson, Mrs Bishop and Mrs Jones into the garden and stay with them."

"Right you are Sir."

"Now let me take you back to the year of 1933. It was in the town of Tonbridge in Kent there was a young girl named Jean Brown. She lived in the cottage at the end of the town. She had a brother and sister. Mr Brown was a very strict chap, what he said you had to do. Jean would do anything to get out of going to chapel. One day she met up with a young man in the castle grounds of Tonbridge, she fell for him hook, line and sinker. Although he was years older than her she knew this was the man for her and she was going to make sure no other girls would get their hands on him. Jean never attended her school when her father was away. She was always out with the boyfriend and her siblings would back her lies. The boyfriend concern worked with his brother on the farm just outside Hadlow. She was with him whenever possible and she was always waiting for him by the farm gate. They were walking back to her cottage when they noticed a fair on the village green."

"Jean begged him to take her to the fair. In the end he gave in and took her on the Saturday evening. On the way home a certain thing took place and she found she was expecting a child, but when her boyfriend found out he washed his hands of her. He never wanted to set eyes on her again. Jean was in a right rage, shouting at him and told him that she always gets anything, just anything she wants. But it was two weeks later when her father found out and he told her to pack her bags and leave. She went to a home for naughty girls and had a child."

"On her return she married a young man who lived in the same street and they moved to a cottage on the coast, in the small town of Rye. It was only after eighteen months that she kicked her husband out, and six months later her husband was tragically killed in a tractor accident. And this woman had the gall to claim off his insurance, she was hoping for an extra-large pay-out. The insurers turned her down flat and then the hatred and resentment started to build in her."

"She had made up of mind that she was going to kill Oswald Jones, the handsome cad who so cruelly discarded her. That was your intention, am I correct Mrs Flyn?" demands the Inspector. "So you started to track him down. The farm was put up for sale and you move to Tonbridge in a small cottage. You then changed your name to Flyn and told everybody that did not know that you came from southern Ireland; there were regular visits around the town letting everybody know that Mrs Flyn arrived. With a bit of luck she thought she had found him, then she found out he had moved on. The talk of the town was that Oswald married a young lady from outside of town. By chance she came across a newspaper article with a photograph of Oswald Jones, and there was a sister she did not know he had who was living in Rye. So, she put her cottage up for a short let and soon found a flat in Rye. There was no time wasted in finding Mrs Jepson, Oswald's sister, who lived close to the harbour."

"The minute she met up with Mrs Jepson the old sob story started, and the tears started to run down her face. You see, Mrs Jepson was a person who would help anybody. Mrs Flyn told her, '*You just know what Oswald was like. One minute he was the nicest man you could meet and two hours later he was a violent, horrible man. He walked out and left me to bring up the young boy on my own without any money and I only have the clothes I'm standing in. I have no place to stay and no money for food.*'"

"Of course, Mrs Jepson said that the poor Mrs Flyn must stay with her. Flyn lays it on thick saying, '*You are so kind. I just don't know what I would have done without you.*' However, it did not take very long for Mrs Flyn to start pinching money. There's a great deal more she stole. One day a distressed Mrs Jepson asked, '*Have you seen my purse? I've hunted high and low I can't find it anywhere.*'"

To which Mrs Flyn callously replied, '*I'm afraid it happens to us all, old-age. You must be suffering from loss of memory Mrs Jepson.*'"

"Then Mrs Flyn started moving things about so Mrs Jepson could not find them and became more confused. In the evening when she was sitting in her armchair, she kept repeating to herself everything and said that she must write her will before her mind goes. The calculating

Flyn offered to help her and the poor Mrs Jepson thought it an act of kindness not suspecting the deception."

"*'Now let me see Mrs Flyn, who did I say I was leaving the cottage to?'* she asked innocently. Flyn then replied *'Mrs Jepson come on get on with it. You said you were leaving the cottage to me, Mrs Flyn.'*"

Under the spell of Flyn, Mrs Jepson said, *'Yes, of course, you are correct. I'm leaving you the cottage and the bulk of my money who was it to?'*"

"*'You said the bulk of your money is going to my son, Alan.'*"

"When Mrs Jepson said she would get her neighbour to witness it, Mrs Flyn told her not to bother herself and she would arrange it for her."

"Picture the scene: Mrs Jepson, having made her will and entrusted the witnessing to Mrs Flyn, lays back in her armchair with a cup of cocoa which has been laced with sleeping tablets by the scheming Flyn. In a dozy state she reveals Oswald Jones' location to Mrs Flyn."

"Now that Flyn has everything she wanted, she no longer has a need for the kind old lady. Without a second thought she smothers her with a pillow and when sure that Mrs Jepson is well and truly dead, Flyn slips away from the cottage quietly like a snake that she clearly is."

"Later back in Tonbridge the following week she buys a local newspaper and the headline in the paper reads, *'Elderly Lady Living Alone In Rye Found Dead'*. Is it not true that the very next day after Mrs Jepson wrote her Will, at breakfast time you kept on at Mrs Jepson to give you the whereabouts of Oswald Jones?"

"Come on Mrs Flyn, out with the truth." growls the Inspector menacingly.

Mrs Flyn whimpers "You see Inspector, at times I get in a very vile temper and I can not control myself. My intention was just to talk things over with Oswald, but my temper got the better of me. It was a big shock to find out Oswald had a twin brother, and you could not tell them apart. I had no idea that Bill Jones had a moustache at the time; someone told me Oswald had a brother but in no way did I know he was a twin."

"Come come Mrs Flyn. You knew he had a brother in the early days, am I correct?"

"Yes Sir. I could not be bothered about his brother, I shut it from my mind. All I wanted was to get my own back on Oswald."

"Not so sure about that Mrs Flyn. Who did Mrs Jepson leave the cottage to?"

" Yes to me Inspector." says Mrs Flyn much quieter and with a sense of resignation, "And yes I already said I knew he had a brother, but having a twin, I'll never get over it. The best thing I could do was to go for a drive which ended in Sandfield Lane. My mind started to get clouded and the whole time I kept thinking it was Oswald Jones. I told him, '*We can get this sorted if we talk things over. How much are you going to give me for bringing up your child?*' He kept on repeating himself, '*My name is Bill Jones, I've never had sex with you and I have no children. I told you over and over again that my name is Bill Jones.*' After he said that so many times I got so wild I hit him hard with a spanner. I then dragged him over to the well and pushed him in. What went on after that you know already Inspector."

"Mrs Flyn, you will be charged with the murders of Mr Bill Jones and Mrs Jepson and the theft by fraud the sum of £120,000." the Inspector says flatly.

As they leave the manor with Mrs Flyn in handcuffs everybody starts to cheer loudly. A number of reporters try to speak to her and take the photos.

~~~

Some days later…

The first thing on the agenda is my brother's funeral. I want to ensure Billy has the absolute best send-off. It will take place here in Wanstead at St John's Church. The Reverend Fox will officiate. Everybody will enter the church with the organist playing Greensleeves, there will be a hymn and prayer. Then we will make our way to the graveside. Rose and Teddy could you do me a very big favour?"

"What is that Oswald?"

"I would like you to stay at the Manor for three of four days. I tell you what, make it two weeks, you have nothing to rush back for."

Rose says, "No we haven't anything important to return for. Teddy and I would love to stay. Oh no!" shouts Rose.

"What's the matter Rose?"

"It's the landlord of the Crow & Bottle. Teddy can you go and have a chat with him?"

He returns twenty minutes later and says "The answer is *yes*, he can get somebody to cover for him."

Stinky tells George, "This time we're going to have an exceptionally good reunion and I'm leaving everything to you and Gerald to arrange. As long as it's like the first one you won't go far wrong. It was a great pity that it started so well and ended up in disaster," Stinky remarks, "But I'm so happy Hilda is back on her feet."

"We all say the same." says Gerald.

"Can you two give me a hand? It's getting a bit too much for me, if we can get the funeral sorted out then I'll be okay. I was hoping that myself, Gerald, George and Fred will carry the coffin from the Manor to the church."

"That's a long way to walk," says George, "but anyway it won't work because Stinky is too short."

Gerald says "Problem solved. The landlord of the Crow & Bottle."

"That's a great idea" agree Stinky and George.

Kitty appears, "Stinky, what about having two black horses and a carriage to the church. Then the four men can take over from the entrance?"

Everyone agrees that's a great idea.

"The Reverend Fox will conduct the service and the organist will play Greensleeves. It was a favourite of Bills and everybody will sing the hymn 'Abide With Me' followed by a prayer. I'll say a few words and then I would like the Reverend Fox to read a poem which was very dear to Bill's heart."

Morning Of The Funeral

Everybody is getting ready for the funeral. Gerald asks what time it starts.

"Forgotten already Gerald!" exclaims George, "It starts at ten-thirty, but we must leave by ten-twenty, not a minute later. By the way Gerald, don't let Jill or Kitty go near Hilda; just leave her to go her own way."

Kitty gently asks Stinky "Is everything going all right?"

"As good as it can Kitty, on a day like today." says Stinky trying his best to remain composed.

"Too true Stinky, too true. We are here for you" Kitty empathises.

Jill asks if anybody would like a cup of coffee before they set off. Kitty and Stinky both say yes. George asks them all to listen for a minute.

"The carriage will be here at ten-twenty; first to leave will be Hilda and Stinky followed by myself and Jill. Then it will be Gerald and Kitty and all the others will follow in pairs behind them. By the way Inspector Platford and Sergeant Moore will attend. It's around fifteen minutes till we go, is everybody ready?"

A little later...

As the mourners make their way into the church the organist is playing Greensleeves. They settle into the pews and Reverend Fox is ready to start.

"Ladies and gentlemen, we are all gathered here today for the funeral of Billy Jones. He was brutishly killed by an evil woman whom he had never met before that fateful evening. Billy was an exceedingly kind person who would not hurt a fly, let us pray that he rests in peace."

"We'll start the hymn, Abide With Me after which we will have a prayer and then just a few words from Oswald Jones."

"What is up? asks Gerald quietly to Stinky. He was to read a poem, but it looks as if he is too upset to carry on. But Stinky steels himself, stands and walks slowly to the pulpit.

In a breaking voice he says, "I would like to read a poem that was very dear to Billy's heart:

"Oh how I would like to sail the seven seas

Stop off at all the tropical islands and see the different kind of trees

Meet all kinds of people from England to Shanghai

Watch the birds from foreign lands flying in the sky

To see all the pretty coloured fish, sharks and wales

Find out in other countries how they all survive

I would have a swim and even have a dive

A walk up the hills and look for miles around

Listening to the church bells ringing in the towns

The wildflowers blazing in the sun

At the top of the hill stands a big old fashioned gun

What a grand time this would be to say

I've sailed across the sea".

After a moments silence. "I would now like to thank everybody from the bottom of my heart for coming to join us in paying our last respects to Billy. Would you all please now make your way to the graveside."

The oak coffin is carried out of the church to the grave, on the coffin is a large cross of dark red roses and a yellow wreath.

After the burial all the mourners make their way back to the Manor. Oswald and Hilda are thanking all those attending the funeral. The

Inspector and Sergeant approach to offer their condolences. The Sergeant tells Oswald and Hilda, "Do you know when we entered the church to the music Greensleeves, it brought back memories of when I lived at Pugshole Farm down Willingford Lane in Burwash Weald."

George says to the Sergeant "Did I hear you say *Pugshole Farm*?"

"Yes you did Mr Stevenson. I lived there for about eighteen months."

"Tell me more Sergeant."

"When I went to school with Eddie May, who lived at Pugshole Farm, Eddie and I attended Burwash School, next to the church. We often passed a house at the top of Willingford Lane, which was on the left, and it was called Greensleeves. Every time I passed it I thought of the music."

"Our teachers at the school were Mr Nutbrown and Mrs White, and the Head Teacher was Mr Downs. Eddie had two schoolmates who were Joe and Ronnie Reeves. We often went to their cottage for tea and to play. They were the nicest boys who attended our school, they had no father, just their mother to bring them up."

The Sergeant goes on, "I tell you now that lady knew how to put on a spread. Where they lived was across two to three acres of fields from the main road. Down the farm where Eddie lived they had a cart horse in the field which we used to jump on, we thought we were riding in the Epsom Derby." he chuckles nostalgically. "Anyway, Eddie and his family moved away in the early fifties and I have no idea where they went. I went up to Surrey and joined a foster family."

Inspector Platford interrupts, "Come on Sergeant Moore we can't stand here all day getting all glassy-eyed."

"Right you are Sir."

Meanwhile Jill and Kitty are busy serving coffee, and George and Gerald serving sherry. Hilda goes over to Rose and Teddy, "Would you like another coffee or glass of sherry?"

"No thank you Hilda, we are happy as we are, thank you."

"Rose could you please tell me where is Tom, the landlord of the Crow & Bottle?"

"Over there in the corner, talking to the landlord of the Royal Oak."

"Thank you Rose."

"Found you two at last. Do you require anything?" offers Hilda to the landlords.

"That's very kind of you but no thank you, we are both okay."

Oswald and Hilda make their way around the lawn thanking everybody again. "We hope to see you all Sunday week for the reunion, thank you all."

"The band is all set up and ready to play." says Oswald. He asks Reverend Fox, "Would you join me with a drink before we start? I'm dying for one, perhaps I should not have used that word Reverend.". A slight grin on the Reverend's face shows he understands Stinky's humour.

The next minute Stinky's calling to Fred and Tom, "Come and join us with a drink." as George and Gerald catch up.

Gerald says, "I have to give in Fred or I'll never last out." Stinky makes his way to the stage followed by the Reverend Fox.

"Good evening ladies and gentlemen." welcomes Stinky "Let's start the evening off by raising your glasses to Bill Jones who recently had a tragic death."

After the toast, "I will now hand you over to Reverend Fox of St John's Church."

"Good evening one and all." Everybody at the reunion claps and cheers. "I won't be able to live this down. This is the second time I've had such a great welcome here. Let's start the evening off with a prayer and then we will sing Onward Christian Soldiers after which we will have a three-minute silence."

After the silence, the Reverend wishes all attending a very enjoyable evening. "And now everybody please join in with Oswald 'Stinky' Jones playing on his banjo, You Are My Sunshine."

Gerald asks George, how many people are going to the potting shed. George says "I've got a full list of people that want to take part. We'll make a start when Stinky finishes playing."

"Plenty of cash on you?" George asks Gerald. "I've got enough to tide me through Gerald."

"Do you know George, I would not have believed it if I had not seen them with my own eyes. Just look over there; Hilda, Jill and Kitty doing the 'CanCan'. As long as they are enjoying themselves that's all that matters."

Stinky returns from the stage and calls out to Bruce Renton, "Are you coming to the potting shed for a bit of how's your luck? A large percentage of the takings are going to the RAF at Hawkinge."

"That's sounds a great idea Stinky." says Bruce.

George joins Rose, Teddy and Tom sitting on an iron seat watching everything going on. "Teddy, I don't think I told you about the folly at Hadlow. Walter Martin May had the castle built, but what year it was built I'm not quite sure. But in the fifties, the council had the castle pulled down and just left some fields and the tower."

"There's a story concerning Walter M May; it goes like this. The word was Walter Martin May believed his wife had run astray, so he built a tower to look out. One day he wonders '*Who is that over by yonder nook'*. He shouts out '*Yes that's them by heck!*' and leaned out a little further but fell and broke his bloody neck. You'll find out he is laid to rest next to Hadlow Church by an old yew tree. The rector will show anybody the grave who would like to see it."

Rose just smiled and Teddy said, "What a poor sod."

Jill and Kitty ask Teddy to go and find out what the others are up to, "It's getting near closing time."

Teddy finds Gerald who tells him, "You know Stinky is a lucky old devil. He has only just won the jackpot, £80!"

"I'm giving £70 of this money to the RAF at Hawkinge." declares a triumphant Stinky.

"Come on then Hilda, come with me up on the stage, I insist. Ladies and gentlemen I would like to thank everybody for coming this evening. We have made a handsome sum of six thousand pounds which is going to the RAF charity. Would everybody join hands and sing 'Auld Lang Syne' and I wish you all a safe journey home, thank you."

"What a beautiful day it has been Simon. But now there is a nasty black cloud heading this way. Its time we made a move and headed for home." says George slowly getting to his feet.

After fifteen minutes walking along the road George sees an old couple in the distance. As they get closer he sees it is Gerald and Kitty. He asks them where they're going. "We came out looking for you and Simon, you've been gone hours. Anyway, Happy Birthday Simon" they reply cheerily.

"That's very kind of the two of you."

The End

Peter May

Peter (aka Edward) May was born in the 1930's in rural Kent and lived a country life as a child in war-torn England. He recalls seeing 'Doodlebug' flying bombs overhead as he played in the fields. Now living in a nursing home in Eastbourne, this is his first book which weaves a gentle crime thriller with some of his own childhood memories of places and people.

.

Printed in Great Britain
by Amazon

57409921R00066